THE
OFFICER'S
HOUSE

THE OFFICER'S HOUSE

JUDITH BALLER-FABIAN

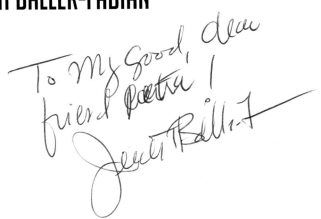

TATE PUBLISHING
AND ENTERPRISES, LLC

Published by Tate Publishing & Enterprises, LLC
127 E. Trade Center Terrace | Mustang, Oklahoma 73064 USA
1.888.361.9473 | www.tatepublishing.com

Tate Publishing is committed to excellence in the publishing industry. The company reflects the philosophy established by the founders, based on Psalm 68:11,
"The Lord gave the word and great was the company of those who published it."

Published in the United States of America

ISBN: 978-1-62994-530-9
1. Fiction / Romance / Time Travel
2. Fiction / Romance / General
14.01.03

For my beloved sister, the original Barbara Ann

ACKNOWLEDGMENTS

SPECIAL THANKS TO my good friend and editor, Karen Judd, who helped me tie up all the loose ends and haunted my dreams with questions like, "Judi, do you really think it would take *three months* to drive from North Carolina to New Jersey in the 1940s?" And to Naomi, Leah and Chris and the warm and welcoming writers' group on East 4th Street, who listened and suggested and supported me through the good times and the bad. Finally, thank you to my husband, Allan, who sat through numerous readings with great patience and good cheer.

The history of World War Two and the Twentieth Century is well documented and available for research. I also used print and online material from state historical associations, the U.S. Department of the interior and the National Park Services. Finally, a shout out to Richard A. Conlan, Visitor Services Coordinator, National Museum of the United States Navy, who kindly answered my query about the tonnage of bombs that fell on Pearl Harbor.

CONTENTS

CHAPTER ONE

SANDY HOOK

AUGUST 15, 2009

A S THE LATE afternoon breeze swept through the house, Emily poured the last of the coffee into a paper cup, brushed her hair back and slipped out onto the veranda to watch the sun set over the water; to see if the strange young woman would be standing by the bay. The sea grass was brown now, dry from the August sun, the water in the bay apathetic, smooth as gray glass, small waves just beginning to ripple with the dusk. The sound of the cicadas was fading to a low, lazy hum. As Emily stood there, her mind began to drift and she felt a slight chill, even in the evening heat. They say your life flashes through your mind when you're drowning, she thought. Am I drowning?

She had come to Manhattan in the spring of 1996, her blond curls, so light they almost looked silver in the sunlight, held back by a red beret; an eager young woman tucked into a window seat on a Greyhound bus. She had gazed at the countryside as they sped up Route I-95, her journalism degree and a sampling of *North Carolina Today* articles tucked into her suitcase, ready to take the big city by storm at *Around the City*, one of New York City's monthly magazines…or maybe a gentle rain?

Emily Craig was quiet, raised by an awkward spinster aunt who loved her dearly and surrounded her with music and art in her small North Carolina home. Auntie Emily was Emily's namesake, something she never failed to tell people, with pride. She also believed "silence is golden," so Emily became a dreamy child who nourished her imagination with daydreams of adventure and romance. Sitting on the bus, as it ground its way through Virginia and Maryland and finally up the New Jersey Turnpike, she believed she was following her dream. She wondered now if she had found her dream, asked herself again as she stood looking across the bay.

She dug at a small, hard ball of new paint on the edge of the porch railing with her fingernail and her mind turned to her husband, God knows where in the mountains of Afghanistan, doing God knows what. Nine-eleven, when it seemed the world had gone mad, Derek had visited the local army recruitment center with two neighborhood men; all three had enlisted in the National Guard in a passion of patriotism. And now he was gone. Again. Gone from his job on Wall Street, gone from his house and gone from her. She hugged herself. I miss you, Derek. Where are you? Are you safe? Are you even alive? She shivered.

She ran her fingers lightly across the railing as her thoughts wandered back to their little house on the mainland, and she sighed. She hadn't been home even once since moving her belongings out to Fort Hancock: to History House with its strange voices and laughter, the soft kiss that would wake her. Her heart jumped and she felt faint when she thought of the young officer in the photograph, his strong body and handsome face. Her mind turned to the indelible chalked August 15th written on the blackboard outside the kitchen. She thought: today is August 15th. I wonder…then lost that train of thought and realized she had almost forgotten her cute Cape-style home with its trim lawns and flowering shrubs, things that she had taken such pride in. With a start she acknowledged that until now she hadn't given a thought to Derek either.

Derek: the love of her life. A chance encounter at a book signing in one of Manhattan's last private bookstores. Eyes across a table of new mystery novels and Emily was lost in his dark-haired good looks, his clear blue eyes that twinkled behind the lenses of his glasses. He had smiled a lopsided smile and she was captivated. By the end of the evening, the handsome Derek and the dreamy Emily left the bookstore together and they never looked back.

He showed her the City: the crowded streets that crept between sky-high office towers, the endless stream of yellow taxis inching up Madison Avenue and down Fifth, the energy that pulsed day and night. They both adored being part of the city's heartbeat, and they walked all the way downtown to the New York Harbor and took a ferry across to the Statue of Liberty. They walked across town to the Empire State Building and rode to the top in an elevator filled with Asian tourists, and for Emily's birthday Derek took her to dinner at Windows on the World, high up on the top floor of the World Trade Center's North Tower, where she felt as if she were flying. Odd, she thought now, there should have been a sign, some hint of what would happen there four years later, maybe the date scrawled on the sidewalk in front of the towers or scratched into the side of a subway car.

She rolled the ball of white paint between her fingers and thought about their wedding at Auntie Emily's small Community Church on the Outer Banks of North Carolina, Derek's parents, with Auntie Emily and Emily's childhood friends, in attendance, beaming, the reception held on the beach. *"This is the beginning of my wonderful life,"* she wrote in her diary, *"and this is the love of my life."*

The next summer they found a small Cape-style house on a quiet dead-end street in Atlantic Highlands, New Jersey, a Victorian town across the water from Manhattan. Derek bought a new white Honda Accord and he and Emily drove to the Atlantic Highlands Terminal each morning to catch the ferry, standing together on the deck to watch for the first sight of the city streets, waiting for the crowded uptown bus to carry them to work in midtown Manhattan. Life was good and when Emily became pregnant, she felt her life had finally found its full meaning.

The breeze picked up a leaf and tossed it into the air, and Emily stuck the paint ball back on the porch railing, squeezing it into a crack in the wood. She remembered the joy she had felt at the thought of the baby, how she and Derek had hugged in front of the bay window, the light streaming through the glass and onto the rug.

By autumn Emily had begun to feel a soft flutter in her belly, like a small butterfly had somehow found a home there. She knew it was her baby telling her hello, and she was enchanted. She started to buy things for the baby: tiny shirts and buntings in yellow and green fleece; small blankets for the crib and a set of tiny dishes with Peter Rabbit and Jemima Puddle-Duck painted in soft pastel colors on each dainty piece. She packed her purchases in a drawer of the dresser, smoothing the soft blankets and baby clothing as she did so. Some evenings she would sit in the nursery with the new crib and matching dresser, rocking and talking softly, singing to her little stranger: *Little baby, little one, Mama's waiting for you to come...* and she knew she would be the mother to her children that she had never known herself.

She recalled that brisk October morning, how she and Derek were getting ready for work, how tired she was when she sat back down on the bed. "I'm staying home, Derek," she told him. "I don't feel like making the trip to Manhattan today. I have sick days saved up. After all, Honey, I'm almost a mother, you know. I think I can take a day off now and then."

Derek had smiled and leaned over, planting a kiss on her blond curls. "You better get as much rest as you can now, Kiddo. That little guy won't let either one of us get any when he gets here."

Emily remembered their quick kiss. "Uh uh, Derek, not little guy, little *girl*," she'd teased him as he'd left for the City. She shivered again as she remembered the rest: by midmorning, she'd felt better, fixed a cup of hot tea, had sat at the kitchen table, gazing out at the blue-and-gold October and humming along with the radio. It was a perfect autumn day and in her memory she could still see the small V of geese as they headed south through the crystal sky; remembered how, as the V broke apart and disappeared, she was suddenly struck by massive pain, doubling her over and sending her to her knees on the kitchen floor, and there, a red drop, like a small ruby and then another one right next to her left knee. Red drops that merged and spun with her sudden storm of tears as she had reached for the phone.

My baby, oh, my poor baby, she thought now, remembering how she had held her belly with both arms, protecting her young one from nature's assault as she waited for the ambulance to come.

In the hospital, as Derek held her and wept, Dr. Adler assured them that this was not unusual, and there would be another baby. But Emily lay frozen, her heart broken. "But not *this* baby, not my poor, poor little one!" And indeed, there were two more pregnancies and two more miscarriages. And things began to change.

Emily looked back through the big front door; immediately her anxious thoughts seemed to still. She moved to the front of the veranda and smoothed her sundress over her hips. As the sun sank toward the bay she searched the seawall for the stranger, the woman who often stood there alone, unapproachable in the setting sun. She thought about the last few months, thought about living alone, about finding the job at Fort Hancock, about how she felt more at home in History House now than in Atlantic Highlands and how she sometimes dreamed about Derek, somewhere in the mountains of Afghanistan; but by the time his unit had been sent to Afghanistan there didn't seem to be any more "Emily and Derek," and, although she would never say it aloud, it occurred to her on more than one occasion that her husband would rather go to war than live in this empty peace at home. However, with his leaving, the house had become lonelier than ever and Emily regretted having left her job and friends the year before, after her third miscarriage. I feel sick with regret, she told herself now, but realized she didn't know what the regret really was for, only that somehow they'd become awkward strangers, this love of her life and her, and now he was gone, somewhere in a war zone.

As the sun sank into the west and shadows were thrown across the lawn, the stranger came around the side of the house and climbed up on the seawall. As usual, she gazed out over the water, her face remote, her long, dark hair ruffled by the breeze.

But this time Emily knew that she would join her.

CHAPTER TWO

EMILY AND DEREK

APRIL 2009

THE WEEK BEFORE Derek's unit was to leave for Afghanistan, Emily's small, second-hand Toyota gave up the ghost. It was now sitting pitifully in the garage by their house. As she had lurched and roared into the driveway, Derek had taken one look and laughed out loud. "Oh, my God, Em, your poor car. Just use mine while I'm gone. It'll save us the cost of repairing yours."

Emily had looked at her beloved blue Toyota as its engine huffed and puffed, shuddered once and finally shut down, and she had to agree. So, the day Derek left with his unit, she rode out to the National Guard field with him in his car, soon to be hers for the next year.

It was still cool for the end of April and a fine rain misted the countryside. Emily looked out the car window for a few minutes, then turned to Derek. "Maybe you should bottle some of this mist to take with you." She looked back at the early spring landscape. From the moment they'd left the house she had avoided the back seat, where his packed duffel sat like a sad, lumpy passenger. Maybe if I don't look at it, this will be some bad dream, she thought.

Derek smiled and glanced at her, then turned back to the highway. "From what I gather, it would take all of a minute in the Afghan sun to dry up a gallon of this rain." He reached over and patted her knee. "And you know what? I'll bet you dollars to donuts that within a month I'll be missing this nasty stuff!" Emily traced a heart on the back of his hand with a finger and looked at him, now whistling softly through his teeth, and wondered: when did we become so awkward with each other?

One of her legs had cramped up and her eyes were sticky with the lack of sleep. All night long she'd curled up next to him as close as she could, resting her head on his chest, listening to his heartbeat as his even breath whispered through his mouth. Oh, my love, my love. Where do we go from here? When the first gray light slipped under the shades, she crept out of bed and padded downstairs to start the coffee, waiting for Derek to shower and change into his uniform.

By the time they arrived at the army reserve base, a crowd had already gathered in the field house. Emily followed her husband as he heaved his duffel bag over his shoulder and started toward a big, two-story cement-and-brick building near the parade ground. People were milling around inside, restless, exhausted.

The field house was one large, high-ceilinged room, painted light mustard with bleachers along two walls and high windows behind iron bars. Offices were located behind the bleachers and all but one were closed, surely locked for the duration. Light leaked out from the half-open door of the open office. Derek dropped his duffel by one of the bleachers. "Watch this for a minute, Em. I gotta check in with Command." He gave her a quick kiss and headed into the crowd. Emily looked down at the duffel bag. It was now just a piece of luggage, not the lumpy, bumpy stranger in their car. She looked around at the families gathered around her and waved as a small, energetic woman came through the crowd, smiling and gesturing frantically.

"Em." Rebecca Wade gave her a quick hug. "This isn't the happiest day, is it? My God, I really didn't think this day would actually come again, but here it is, here it is!" She fanned herself with an army wives' brochure and looked around.

Emily nodded, a lump in her throat. Rebecca's husband was Derek's second in command, his closest friend. Roger Wade worked on Wall Street, owned a big colonial house in the next town and often had barbecues in the large backyard. There was also a gang of rowdy Wade children who spent the evenings roughhousing in the backyard, where their games would often escalate into loud, roaring fights. Rebecca would calmly pull them apart with a sharp "enough!" and march one or two of them into the house for a "time-out." Emily could never figure out how many children there were. She would leave the Wades' feeling relieved that she actually *didn't* have a gang of children of her own.

She managed a small smile. "I have dreaded this day, too! I feel pretty numb. I certainly don't look forward to going home to an empty house again either." She swallowed hard and rubbed her eye with one finger.

Rebecca looked at her with understanding and slipped an arm around her shoulder again. "Oh, Honey, I agree, and I if I didn't have a doctor's appointment today, I would take you home with me." Patting her stomach, Rebecca whispered, "Another Baby Wade may be on the way. I have to stand near the exit so I can leave as soon as the men do, or, God forbid, I suddenly throw up. I'll call you tomorrow."

"Seriously?" Emily looked at her friend in amazement. "How in the world do you ever manage it?" She didn't know whether she envied her friend or felt sorry for her, but she laughed and then turned to look across the room. "I see Derek coming, Becca. Before we all get swept away, please, let's plan to always keep in touch, a new Baby Wade or not."

"Of course! *We two gotta stick together*," Rebecca sang sotto voce and gave her another quick squeeze before turning away. She blew Derek a kiss as she breezed back across the floor and disappeared in the crowd. "Derek, good luck and you boys keep each other safe."

Emily watched her friend as she threaded her way through the crowd. She envied her confidence. It seemed as if all of hers had drained away over the past year since she'd stopped working. Derek picked up his duffel bag and put his arm around her. "We need to move outdoors in a few minutes, Honey…I have to go join my unit." He looked at her and frowned, his blue eyes serious. "I just hate knowing that you'll be alone, that you'll worry or be scared. I don't like leaving you like this. I feel so, so sad."

Emily managed a smile. "Becca and I will be keeping in touch and I should be finding a job soon. Who knows, I may swallow my pride and see if the magazine would take me back freelance. I do have my yoga, you know, and the house, so I imagine I won't have much time to be scared…or lonely. Please, just take care of yourself, don't do anything foolish or valiant, don't be…uh… *heroic!*"

Derek wrapped his arms around her and she buried her face in his shoulder. As he held her and kissed her good-bye, she closed her eyes and sent a silent prayer: Please, whatever might be the future, whatever happens between the two of us, just bring Derek home safe.

The unit had planned a farewell ceremony and the families huddled together in the April dawn. The troops marched in neat columns across the parade ground, uniforms clean and pressed, medals polished and chevrons aligned. Emily stood with the other families, smiling wanly and waving in the drizzle. Across the field, she could see Rebecca's tousled head bobbing back and forth as she watched the ceremony. And then they were gone, families watching as the military transports bumped back onto the Garden State Parkway and then south to Fort Dix and McGuire Air Force Base. With much blowing of noses and wiping of eyes, the crowd slowly drifted away, gathering at cars and vans. Emily stood alone in the drizzle, looking for Rebecca and hoping for another few minutes with her friend. She thought: And so Emily Craig is alone…

"Emily Craig!" An elegant blond waved and sent her an air kiss. "We were wondering if you would be here." She weaved her way between the puddles and made a beeline for Emily, a few of her groupies following close behind. These were The Officers' Wives (Emily always emphasized the first word), the New Jersey Clique who never missed an event or gathering where they could show off their husbands' silver bars and gold maple leaves, sipping wine and looking around for next waiter, the next full glass, these women with French or Irish au pairs who had never held a job. Unless you were to count the various charities or political party activities, Emily thought.

She smiled stiffly. And why would I not be here? she wondered sourly to herself, but then softened her expression. "Ladies." She joined the women as they headed back inside. Coffee had been supplied in the field house and was still hot and the women sat together, sipping from the heavy white mugs as the light rain let up and the day brightened.

"When shall we meet," a tall redhead drawled, her eyes darting around the group. "Where should we hold our first officers' wives' luncheon? Emily, you *will* join us. You are one of us, of course!" and Emily thought snidely: Yeah, even if I am a working wife.

She smiled. "Of course. Thank you, Ladies." She looked around for Rebecca, but she'd already left. darn! I could use a little more of Becca right now and a little less of the "Officers' Wives of New Jersey." How can I stand this? How can I ever stand this? I'm going home!

Later Emily stood in the empty front hall, her bag hanging off her shoulder, her keys dangling from her right hand, then tossed them on the hall table and looked around. She had loved this little house from the moment she'd seen it years before, but suddenly it didn't seem familiar. "What?" she asked out loud, just to hear her voice. "Hello, House." Then, "What?"

She dropped her bag on the hall table and wandered into the kitchen. Coffee? Tea? She picked up the teapot and filled it with water from the tap, plopped it on one of the burners. As she waited for the water to boil, she looked out at the backyard with its new green grass, the forsythia buds just turning gold in the sunshine. "Crap," she said out loud and dropped a teabag in one of the mugs and added the boiling water. "Crap," she said again, then, "crap, crap, *crap!*" She looked around her bright, cozy kitchen and suddenly the emptiness seemed as loud as a shout and the home that she loved as silent as a tomb.

For the first two weeks after Derek's leaving, Emily woke at first light, spending a few minutes gazing around the bedroom. She'd open the big windows to the early dawn, then wander into the shower, standing under the spray, soaping herself and washing her hair until the short tendrils squeaked. After the soapy water disappeared down the drain, she'd carefully wrap herself in a soft towel and brush her blond curls until they bounced around her face. Emily was stunning; white-blond curls framed a heart-shaped face and blue eyes fringed by Elizabeth Taylor eyelashes. Auntie Emily disapproved of "preening" and even now she could hear her voice in her head: "Pretty is as pretty does, Emily." Derek had told her she was beautiful, but now, as she looked at herself in the bathroom mirror every morning, she would study the delicate face with its blue eyes and arched eyebrows and wonder if she would ever feel beautiful again. Who are you? Who are you, Emily? What ever happened to Derek and Emily?

As the days went by, the morning ritual became familiar: shower, makeup, hair, dress, and before breakfast, a quick look at the Internet to check any messages from Derek, then into the kitchen for breakfast. Every morning she nervously glanced over the international section of the *New York Times* and quickly read the reports from the Middle East. Only then would she relax with the local news and employment pages. Day after day she would fold the paper back up and think, what to do, what to do?

The first day she cleaned the house from top to bottom and did a load of laundry. The second day she started again, and then gave up. How clean can it be? she wondered. Can one person mess up a whole house in one day? "Well, you just don't," she told herself out loud.

After a week she came to the conclusion that the best solution was to find another job, even in the dreadful job market. She put up a small bulletin board she'd bought in a yard sale in some past summer day trip, found a few tacks in a kitchen drawer and carefully printed *Get A Job* on a slip of paper and tacked it to the board. Each day she would glance at the paper on the bulletin board and vow to start looking. But, so far, checking the employment pages was the best she was able to do. "Rats," she'd say and then go start the coffee pot and set a single place at the table; the loneliness was like an ache deep in her bones.

CHAPTER THREE

ADALET'S APRON

APRIL 2009

EMILY LOVED YOGA, and she and Derek had joined a local gym in Atlantic Highlands. She was convinced that yoga would help prevent a miscarriage and she faithfully attended class on Tuesday and Thursday evenings. Much to her sorrow, it didn't help with the pregnancies, but it did seem to help a bit with her state of mind.

The Tuesday after Derek left, she picked up her yoga mat and bag and headed for the gym. Her friends Jena and Ruthie were waiting for her at the door to the studio. They had said their good-byes as well: Ruthie to her husband; Jena to a good friend and roommate, and they spent the class somberly, lotus-style, trying to lose themselves in the quiet and peace of the moment. The younger women watched, furtively, wondering, whispering: "How would I act, not knowing? Should we say something or not? But what should we say? I'm sorry? Everything will be OK? A year really isn't a long time?"

After the three women showered and dressed, they strolled to Adalet's Apron, a tearoom owned by a stout and youthful Turkish woman named, aptly, Adalet, who offered home-baked cookies and sweet rolls, Turkish coffee, and a variety of teas. The Apron was an attractive, cozy place with a big window that looked out over the main street. A number of small, round tables were placed around the room, two chairs pulled up to each and colorful posters of Turkish villages and landscapes on the wall. A glass case displayed the day's offerings, and a silver-and-brass coffee machine puffed quietly on a counter behind the pastry case. Emily pulled another chair up to one of the little round tables and, dropping their yoga gear by their chairs, the three friends sat down and looked woefully at each other. Adalet came over, smiling. "What to have, Ladies?" she asked in softly accented English.

"Sweet rolls, tea," they chorused and Adalet looked down at them with understanding in her brown eyes."

The men, they are gone, no?" she asked. "I'm so sorry and I'll bring such nice sweet rolls as gift for you ladies."

Adalet's thoughtfulness touched Emily and brought tears to her eyes. She watched as Adalet readied their order at the counter, then brought their drinks and sweet rolls and set them on the table. Emily touched one of the cups. "Derek left for Afghanistan last week. He'll be gone for a year and I really don't know what to do without him. Funny, huh? I thought I'd be OK. But now I'm not so sure."

Adalet patted her shoulder and clucked like a mother hen. "I know what is like, the war. I remember so many troubles in my Turkey. In 1980, my husband, we leave when almost a civil war happened and we came to America."

After Adalet left the table, the three friends sat in silence as they shared the sweets and tea. "What will you do now?" Jena asked, addressing both of her friends. Emily sighed.

"I need to find a job. I keep looking in the paper, but all I can find are high-tech positions, nothing at all in publishing. I thought about trying to get my old job back, but can't seem to get myself in gear. In fact," she admitted, "I feel awful." She sighed again and picked up her teacup.

Ruthie nodded in agreement. She had been a successful bond trader below Wall Street but had seen her job disappear like smoke the year before. She leaned back in her chair and picked up the conversation. "Nothing," she said with disgust, and tossed her dark braid back over her shoulder. "I've been looking every day and so far? Nada!" She took a healthy bite of her sweet roll and chewed sullenly.

"Well," Jena said, "I'm going back to school to learn barbering. I can't see myself shuffling papers around in a stuffy old law office forever and now with this recession, no telling how long that will last, anyway."

"What?" Emily choked and swallowed her tea. "You want to be a *barber*? Like in a man's barbershop?"

Ruthie and Emily looked at each other in amazement. Neither of them could imagine their little blond, baby-doll friend slicing away at men's hair day after day. Emily immediately had a vision of her working in a small, messy barbershop with a red-and-white barber pole turning lazily by the front door.

"Wait," Jena interrupted, "it's very stylish these days. With long hair or…ah…no hair. It's all very in now!"

Emily laughed and then sat back in her chair. "Darn it, here I am, feeling sorry for myself and just looking at the want ads every day. You go out and find yourself a whole new career. You embarrass us, Jena." But the very idea was enough to give her encouragement.

The three women thanked Adalet and waved good-bye as they left, walking slowly through the early evening dusk. At the parking lot they loitered for a few minutes, hating the idea of their empty houses, but all the way home Emily laughed to herself as she imagined Jena Rose, standing on a stepladder, cutting the hair of some big bear of a man wearing a red plaid shirt and sporting a long beard. However, it did remind her that she needed to find something sooner than later. The bills were beginning to pile up on the kitchen table.

Every day Emily picked up the mail with dread. She'd receive Derek's pay at the end of the month, but the bills came every day: the phone bill one day and the cable and electric bill the next. Each one joined the others piled on the table. When Derek was at home, he took care of the bills and budget. Emily hated this responsibility and it always made her nervous when he was gone. Each afternoon she sat at the kitchen table and carefully sliced the envelopes with a letter opener, slipped the bills out and smoothed them on the table in front of her.

I think I'll keep a record, she told herself and found a notebook in one of Derek's desk drawers. I'll write the name and amount down in the notebook. Then I'll mark it off as soon as it's paid. The idea cheered her and she set to work with a ruler and pencil, making careful columns on the pages.

But the columns remained empty and before the end of the month, Emily knew that she would have to raid their savings account to pay the bills. "Rats," she said after jotting down another three bills. "I need to find a job."

CHAPTER FOUR

BETTY

NORTH CAROLINA 1931

BETTY WILSON WAS sixteen when she met James Warren. Her mother was elbow deep in flour and sugar when she suddenly stopped and looked at the bowl in alarm, then turned to Betty, who was sitting at the kitchen table with her chin in her hand, gazing idly out the window.

"I have no eggs! Here I am in the middle of cake-making and I don't have one single egg to my name. Betty, take some change from my purse and run down to Burrows's Farm and see if you can weasel an egg or two from Mr. Burrows."

It was 1931 and now the Depression that had started in 1929 was beginning to take its toll. Getting an egg or two was not an easy task, so Betty sighed and rolled her eyes. "Oh, *Mother.* Why do I have to go all the way down there and try to get eggs from Mr. Burrows? He's a grumpy old man!"

Her mother dusted the flour off her hands. "Stop whining and get a move on, young lady, and take Scout with you. That dog of yours needs a nice long walk."

Betty slid out of the kitchen chair and headed out the back door, whistling to Scout as she slammed the screen door behind her. Not that she was a lazybones, by any means, but she really didn't like to go ask Mr. Burrows for anything at all. He was always angry these days and not at all like he had been when she'd been a child. As she started down the road to town, she smiled at a sudden memory.

She'd been what…ten years old? Times were pretty hard in the small North Carolina town, even before the Depression started, and people didn't have a lot of money. Betty's father was the only doctor in Swansboro, and people came from far and wide when they needed medical help. Sometimes, if they had no money, they brought vegetables, a basket of fruit or eggs. It was shortly after her tenth birthday, and her mother decided it was time for the doctor to "close up shop" and come back to the kitchen for supper. She found Betty sitting on the back porch, and, as usual, Betty was sent on the errand. "Betty, please run up front and tell your father to shake a leg and finish up his appointments or supper is sure to get cold. And…hold up there, young lady, stand up straight or you'll grow up crooked!"

Betty skipped through the dining room and down the front hall to her father's clinic and then stopped short at the sound of chairs crashing to the floor and a woman's voice. "Catch it, catch it! Oh my, oh my heavens! We'll all be pecked to *death!* Somebody do something! Help, help! Oh, my poor heart!"

Betty opened the door a crack and slapped her hand over her mouth to keep from laughing out loud. Furniture had turned over and Mrs. Daley, Swansboro's elderly librarian, was standing on a chair, giggling, with her skirts hiked up and her knickers showing. Her father and Mr. Burrows were roaring with laughter as they chased a small brown hen around the office. Betty slipped into the clinic, quickly cornered the hen by the front window and scooped her up in her arms, smoothing her feathers and talking softly.

"Henrietta, that's what I'm going to name her. Daddy, look how cute she is, all brown and soft and just look at her pretty feathers. I *love* her!" She looked up at her father with longing eyes, the hen held tight, and who could refuse her?

As her father told it over supper that evening: "Mr. Burrows is having a hard time, you know. He tries to take care of himself, but he had a touch of that stomach grippe that's going around and had to come in for some tonic."

Betty started to laugh at the memory and her father smiled at her and winked.

"He brought a chicken to barter, a *live* chicken, mind you, which of course escaped from its cardboard box and started running around the waiting room. Scared old Mrs. Daley almost to death, but she's a tough old bird herself, you know." He chuckled, took a sip of water. Betty bounced in excitement.

And so, Henrietta lived to a ripe old chicken age in a coop that Betty and her father built in the backyard, Mrs. Daley had a story to tell for years to come and Mrs. Wilson had no need of Mr. Burrows's eggs. She always had them on hand...out in the backyard.

Now times had changed and Mr. Burrows didn't laugh anymore. He still had chickens and sold eggs but he scared Betty because he would shake his head and grumble to her about the "terrible state of affairs." "Just mark my words, Missy, there will be another Great War and right on top of this Depression. Things are getting worse every day and just you wait, we'll be calling this the Great Depression one day soon. Yes siree, Bob!"

Betty would shuffle her feet in the dust and mumble, "hmm, hmm." She didn't really know what was so great about a war and a depression anyway and she certainly didn't want anybody to come to Swansboro, North Carolina, and drop bombs. The world was becoming a very scary place, but very soon she would not be scared of Mr. Burrows anymore because of a boy named James.

CHAPTER FIVE

THE OFFICERS' WIVES

APRIL 2009

THE THIRD WEEK of April was warm, the sides of the road misted with yellow forsythia. Tiny green leaves began to fill the bushes in the yard, and in the garden a few crocuses appeared overnight. A few warm showers in the early mornings cleared by noon.

One morning Emily's cell phone gave a startled chirp and began a dance on the counter. A cheerful voice announced: Valerie Marley, "one of the *older* officers' wives from the National Guard unit. You know, the Grandmothers Club?"

"Emily," she continued, "I'm calling to see if you'd like to meet with some of us for lunch tomorrow. I know it's short notice, but we like to get together every week or so and, you know…talk things over, what with the 'little boys' gone."

Oh, Lord, Emily thought, little boys? But…maybe it will help to get out, to meet some of the other wives. "How nice of you to think of me," she said. "Let me just check my calendar." She held the phone in her hand and looked out the window for several seconds while she drank in the sunlight and new spring growth, then noisily rustled the pages of the calendar that hung by the refrigerator next to the phone. After a few more seconds she picked up again. "It looks like I'm free for lunch," she said cheerfully and agreed to join the ladies for lunch the next day.

As she copied down the directions and hung up, Emily felt an unexpected sense of gloom. Blah, she told herself, blah, blah, *blah!* I would rather cut men's hair! But, she consoled herself, at least it's not Blondie and her New Jersey Toadies! She picked up the dishtowel again.

At five o'clock she changed her mind. Why should I sit and listen to those women boast about their grandchildren? I'll call and cancel tomorrow morning. She poured a mug of tea and sat hunched on the kitchen stool, pulled her sweater sleeves over her hands and held the steaming tea up to her face. At bedtime, she changed her mind again. What the heck. I'll go! It won't kill me to spend some time with them and they were kind to invite me. That decided, she pulled down the covers and climbed into bed. The lunch would change her life.

Emily turned her car down a side street and found a place to park in front of a small café. As she pulled into the space, she could see the three women through the café window, smiling and chatting with each other. All of them were older, past retirement age, had grown families and grandchildren. She thought they were very thoughtful to invite her to join them, but for all of their kindness, she really had little in common with any of them. Oh, boy, she thought as she slid out of the car, this is really not how I would like to spend the day. But…whatever. She popped four quarters into the parking meter and walked through the art deco door.

"Oh, Emily, over here." Valerie Marley was the oldest woman in the group and had taken control of the lunches and get-togethers. She was tall and fit. Short gray hair in an expensive cut fell in a smooth curve to each side of her elegant jaw. She stood up and offered an empty seat. The other two smiled and politely rose until Emily had taken her place. Once settled, Valerie turned to Emily, her blue eyes bright and friendly.

"Look," she said, "I know this came as a surprise and you really don't enjoy getting together with all us Oldies but Goodies…No, no, I understand," she waved her hand as Emily tried to interrupt, "but I wanted you to come today because, well, Jane Rider just received a call from a friend down near Sandy Hook." Again, she waved away Emily's embarrassed denial and continued, "Her friend, actually he's a friend of her sister's brother-in-law, anyway, he knows a park ranger at Fort Hancock who's looking for someone as a summer guide in the museum there. I thought of you right away. I heard you were going to look for a job now." She smoothed her napkin, smiled at the group, and continued. "I thought this would be just lots of fun to do. In fact, if I were a hundred years younger, I'd be tempted myself." She leaned back and chuckled.

Jane Rider leaned across the table. "Emily, listen, I think you'd get a kick out of this. Fort Hancock is a noncommissioned army fort and they're sprucing it up as a national park. Most of the officers' houses are in pretty bad shape, but one or two of them are okay." She smiled at Emily and continued. "One is being used by the Southern New Jersey Audubon Society as their headquarters, and the other has just been refurbished as a museum called the History House. You would not *believe* what it's like, all nineteen-forties, just like in World War Two. I just know this would be a real kick for you to do." Jane was a kind woman, short and rather stout with soft light brown hair, a sweet face and kind brown eyes and she almost bounced with eagerness.

Emily was touched by their interest and the more she thought about it the more enthusiastic she became. She looked from Jane to Valerie and back to Jane. "Well, yeah, that does sound like fun and I sure do need to get a job to tide us over. I've been checking the *New York Times* every day since Derek left, and this is a horrid job market, has been for a while. It's depressing."

Jane reached into a rather large handbag that was draped over the chair and handed Emily a piece of notepaper. "Here's the phone number for the ranger, John Rogers. He's in charge of Fort

Hancock and will be the one who will interview you. You'll like each other."

Emily studied the phone number, then tucked it into her jacket pocket and thanked Valerie and Jane. The waitress arrived with the menus and for the rest of the luncheon the three other women talked about the war in the Middle East, their "little boys," the spring weather. As the conversations buzzed quietly in the background, Emily tackled her fruit salad and let her mind drift to the possibility of a job in the strange officer's house at the far end of Sandy Hook.

CHAPTER SIX

BETTY

NORTH CAROLINA 1931-1935

BETTY TURNED AWAY from the waterfront. The sun reflected off the water where the shrimp trawlers were lined up in the bay, their nets hanging from the framing that reached up to the sky like arms. She skipped a few steps and then waited for Scout while he prowled around in the brush. "Come on, boy, let's shake a leg and get this egg business over with as quickly as we can."

She stopped to admire a large, elegant Victorian home adorned with gingerbread and curlicues and sporting a poet's tower off to one side of the wide veranda. It sat on the edge of town and belonged to the new president of the National Bank in Swansboro, a strange man who had come to Swansboro from "Up North" and who spoke with a weird, clipped accent and laughed in a tight-lipped way: "tee hee hee!"

"So, Miss Wilson, what brings you this way?"

Betty jumped and grabbed at Scout's collar as he made a beeline toward the front gate and the young man leaning against one of the posts. She held on to Scout as he licked the stranger's hand, and she smiled shyly and looked around.

"I'm going to buy eggs at Mr. Burrows's farm. Do you live in this house? Are you the new banker's son?" She turned back and stared at the stranger, felt her heart skip a beat.

"Yeah, I'm the banker's son...hoity toity, la di da." He unwound his tall, lanky body and squatted down and scratched Scout's head. "Nice dog. A water spaniel, huh? Nice color, nice coat. Oh, by the way, my name is James. Not Jim, not Jimmy. James! James Warren."

James was good looking, in a tall, blond, lazy blue-eyed way, with a wide, smiling mouth. She thought he was the handsomest boy she had ever seen, even with his weird accent and formal name. In fact, she had to admit, she liked his formal name. Different from Billy Cooper and Tommy Anderson, boys at school...hmm, sounded sort of, well, exotic. "How did you know my name? Will you be going to school here in Swansboro?" She stopped, caught her breath. "Do you want to go to Burrows's farm with me? I don't like to go there. Mr. Burrows is grumpy and talks about war and scary stuff."

James laughed and stood up, stretched lazily and started walking beside Betty. "Gosh, you sure ask a lot of questions, Miss Wilson. So, here goes: I know your name because I asked the librarian when I saw you with your father in town the other day. He *is* the doctor, you know." He laughed again and his eyes crinkled up in a most attractive way. Betty's heart skipped another beat. "You're the doctor's daughter. Yes, I'll be going to high school in Swansboro. I'm seventeen and I'll be a senior. And, yes, I'll go and protect you from the mean, scary Mr. Burrows."

That was the summer that Betty Wilson met James Warren. He protected her from Mr. Burrows's scary stories and she showed him the town. They explored the wharfs with the fishing fleets and shrimpers, where he enjoyed talking to the rough, smelly fishermen and helped empty buckets of fish and shrimp into big coolers.

By September, the doctor's daughter and the banker's son had become a couple and they stayed true to each other all that year and later: when James went off to Middlebury College in Vermont to study foreign languages and European history and when Betty was sent off to secretarial school in Winston-Salem, the next year, to learn to type sixty words a minute and take Gregg shorthand, where the girls wore white gloves and hats whenever they went to town.

Betty and James were married in June of 1935 and moved to the mountains of Asheville, North Carolina, where James taught French and Italian in Asheville Senior High School and Betty happily settled into the small, bright apartment James found for them. This was the place where she wanted to live with James and the family they would start soon. But with the clouds of war gathering on the horizon, this was not to be.

CHAPTER SEVEN

JOHN ROGERS

APRIL 2009

J OHN ROGERS HAD joined the National Park Service shortly after graduating from the University of Massachusetts and was well aware that he cut a handsome figure in his crisp green uniform with its official patch on the sleeve; so it was no surprise to him when he managed to bowl June Moss over in short order. What *was* a surprise to John was that June, with her blond hair and bright blue eyes, had bowled *him* over as well. She had been taking her third-grade class to Morristown National Historical Park, where Rogers was assigned, stopped by the front gate to ask directions and by the end of the day, as she herded her charges into the small bus for the ride back to the Jersey Shore, John and June were making plans for the future. Shortly thereafter, he had asked for and received a transfer to a park closer to the love of his life, and that happened to be Gateway National Park at Sandy Hook and its Fort Hancock venture.

Now, ten years later and a number of pounds heavier, John Rogers sat in his office and studied the résumé in front of him. It was not that he disliked Sandy Hook. "Oh, no," he'd told June the night before. "It's a lovely place and so close to the ocean." What he *didn't* tell her was that he was spooked baby-sitting the old officer's house with its WWII-era furniture, big rooms and creaks and groans. He was forever dashing out to the hallway to see if someone had arrived only to find it empty, strange footsteps fading away across the upstairs floor. To make matters worse, although he had never seen anyone, recently he had started to have the prickly sensation that someone was watching him. About this he never breathed a word. Of course, he reminded himself, that doesn't scare me a bit. What am I, some namby-pamby? Really, give me a break! Just boring, being out here, that's all. However, he decided to hire Emily Craig sight unseen. As long as she has a half a wit about her and is well spoken, of course.

"In fact," he squared the corners of the forms in front of him, even if she *doesn't*. "Enough is enough," he told himself firmly. The ranger squeezed his chubby body around the desk and picked up a feather duster that had been dropped on the floor, doing a last-minute dusting in his tiny office. Waiting for Emily Craig.

Emily drove over the Highlands Bridge that led onto Sandy Hook, turned north on Hartshorne Drive toward Fort Hancock. Before Jane Rider had told her about the place, she'd never heard of Fort Hancock and was curious about this old army camp. Deserted and decommissioned in the 1970s, it was now being turned into a military museum. She would be the summer guide through one of the original officers' houses. This was intriguing and she looked forward to the interview, seeing what her responsibilities would be. *If* she were hired, she reminded herself. This thought lifted her spirits and she hummed along with a Norah Jones CD that was playing softly.

Hartshorne Drive was lined on one side with stunted pines and sea grass that ran along the beach way. Sandy paths led through the trees to the ocean. Here and there a restaurant climbed among the dunes and next to one a small sign announced *The Sea Gull's Nest*. Along the road parking lots were empty and then the ocean, rolling onto the sand. A few hardy souls walked on the shore in the late April sunshine and Emily shivered. The other side of the road faced the western bay: a few hot dog stands still closed for the season and picnic tables scattered along the sand.

Emily had grown up on the Outer Banks in North Carolina and had spent her life on the beaches nearby. She was familiar with the early spring feel of the beach towns, their closed and boarded shops and cafes. When the summer heat struck, the paths and beaches would be packed in the long, hot afternoons and she would share the main road with bumper-to-bumper traffic. Now the road was empty and she had no trouble finding her way to the main gate to Fort Hancock. She stopped at the front gate and following his directions, drove onto the grounds of the fort, turning onto the post road.

The first buildings that came into view were barracks: rows of wooden buildings, long and low, lined with shuttered windows and painted a worn and peeling light yellow, standing empty, facing the ocean side of the fort. Tall pine trees grew among the buildings and threw shadows across their walls and the top of a light house could be seen in the distance. Emily followed the road past the barracks and began to feel transported back to another time and place. The road continued past the barracks and around a large parade ground. A groundskeeper was perched on a small mower cutting grass. Up ahead were old wooden-frame office buildings, ladders leaning against the sides. Everything was in the process of rebirth with paint, shutters and mowers, and a certain excitement was in the air.

At the end of the road, Emily saw the officers' quarters and caught her breath. Standing guard on Sandy Hook Bay, the large brick houses marched in a row. Built to face the western bay, their backs were turned to an open field and the parade ground. These were strange and fascinating homes and Emily was enchanted. Cement stoops led up to the back doors and, on some, small garages were attached. The houses were huge, with large windows on all three floors, wide front verandas open to the breezes off the bay. The bricks were dull yellow, faded. Tall grass grew along the foundations. A dusty street ran down the back of the houses and past the parade ground, another paved street ran in front along the seawall. An old street sign with a faded "Officers' Row" leaned drunkenly on the corner. Even in such disrepair, the big homes were in remarkably good shape, a testament to their late nineteenth-century builders. Even beautiful. Nice, Emily said to herself. Old, but nice, or as Valerie says, "Oldies but Goodies!"

CHAPTER EIGHT

BETTY

ASHEVILLE 1935-1939

ETTY WAS HAPPY in Asheville. She loved the soft, pine-scented air and the lavender mountains that stood guard over the town, and she was pleasantly surprised to find she never missed the ocean at all. She wrote to her parents often and in one of her first letters told them she hoped she and James would live in Asheville forever:

> I can't tell you how much I love living in this town. It's tucked into a valley between the most magical mountains, green and purple and gray. Sometimes the mist hangs over them and it looks like a fairyland.

Little James was born in 1938, a strong and healthy baby. James was delighted and moved the crib into the dining room next to the table in the evening while he corrected class papers. Mrs. Wilson came to Asheville by Greyhound bus to help when Betty came home from the hospital and she was amused at James' doting "like a mother hen."

"Like Henrietta," Betty laughed.

However, Betty and her mother also talked about the troubles: the Depression and the terrible dust storms and drought out west. Times were very cruel and her mother often reminded her how lucky she and James were.

"Thank heavens James has a job, Betty," she'd say. "You can thank your lucky stars you aren't in some old, broken-down car looking for a job far away. My goodness, you could have married Billy Cooper and ended up picking grapes in California."

"Perish the thought, Mother," Betty would groan, "don't even think things like that! Anyway, Daddy says President Roosevelt is trying to fix things. Putting people to work. I'm sure things will get better soon."

But even with the new government jobs that were created, the Depression seemed to drag on forever. Betty and her neighbors started to fix simple meals for the poor souls who would knock on the back door looking for something to eat. Sometimes, James would hire one of the scruffy tramps to cut the lawn or paint the fence and would pay them what money he had to spare, only to find the man had been an accountant in Connecticut or a rancher in Texas. But life went on in Asheville, watched over by the gentle lavender mountains.

But by 1939, James was becoming alarmed at the news from Europe, listened to the radio in the evening, his face grim. "This is not good, Betty, not good at all. The world seems to have lost its mind and I worry about you and Little James."

"Stop, James." Betty would look away and wring her hands. "It reminds me of Mr. Burrows, how he scared me with his war talk."

But James would give her a vague smile and turn back to the news. "I feel like I should be doing something. I studied languages and European history. That should be valuable these days. Maybe my country can use me."

And finally he did do something. At the end of 1939, as the United States Army was building up their forces for the first time since WWI, he joined the Army Officers' Corps and left for six weeks of basic training as a second lieutenant. A heartbroken Betty kissed him at the Asheville bus station, then went home to pack up their belongings and close the little house in the North Carolina mountains and headed back to Swansboro to wait for James to receive his orders.

CHAPTER NINE

THE OFFICER'S HOUSE

APRIL 2009

THE FIRST HOUSE on Officers' Row was in a state of repair: the grass cut neatly along the base and new cement steps to the back door with a stout iron railing running up one side. The bricks were being steam cleaned, and freshly painted shutters, along with an attractive sign that announced *Welcome to History House*, leaned against the side of the house. Someone had scrawled the number *24* on the wall beside the door. Could this be my new place of employment? Emily wondered.

She parked the car on the side of the street behind a green Ford pickup truck with the National Parks seal on the door, climbed out and paused for a moment. Combing her fingers through her light blond curls and smoothing her sweater, she glanced over her right shoulder toward the northern end of Fort Hancock, then mounted the steps to the small back porch and knocked on the screen door. While she waited, she glanced through the screen at a long, dark hall. A door on the right led to a kitchen. Across the hall another door opened to a small office. A small blackboard was hanging on the wall outside the kitchen, along with a group of old photographs and some notices on a corkboard. A short, stout, rather handsome man suddenly popped out of the office and headed down the hall, opened the screen door and welcomed her into the house.

He was about Emily's age and sported a rumpled green uniform with an open collar. His hair was light brown and trimmed so short that it was almost nonexistent... Did he go to Jena for that haircut?

Friendly eyes peered at her through silver-rimmed glasses. He offered his hand and introduced himself. "Ms. Craig, I'm John Rogers, ranger and Manager of Employment at the Gateway National Recreation Area."

Emily smiled back, "Thank you for seeing me, Mr. Rogers. What a fascinating place. Very different." She looked down the hall and through the kitchen door to illustrate her interest.

"John, please, and, yes, it's interesting. Uh...very interesting indeed." He smiled and Emily followed him into a small, cluttered office, taking a chair that faced a large, neat desk. "Make yourself comfortable and I'll give you a little background on Fort Hancock and History House."

While John Rogers squeezed behind the desk and dropped into a rolling office chair, Emily glanced around the room. To her left was one of the large windows that looked out over the open field. Limp green curtains framed the window, a beige shade drawn halfway. A green file cabinet was pushed against the wall with a small cactus plant in a Mexican pot, a pile of books, papers, a glass jar and, oddly enough, a large feather duster on top. A framed photo of a young, blond woman with a small girl sat on the corner of the desk, John Rogers's wife and daughter. The air was stuffy; dust danced in the sunlight.

Emily glanced back at John and found him gazing at her, his chin resting in one hand. Her résumé was centered on the desk, a file of employee forms, attached with a paper clip, lying next to it. He cleared his throat and smiled again.

"Anyway, Fort Hancock was built here on the north end of Sandy Hook Peninsula to provide defense for New York Harbor, which it did from 1895 until it was decommissioned in 1974." He stopped and glanced out the window. "Ironically the Sandy

Hook Lighthouse, which is right up there," he waved a hand in the general direction of the kitchen, "was defended by British Loyalists during the American Revolution to ensure British ships a safe passage into New York City. "But…" he paused for affect and continued importantly, "Fort Hancock itself was a strategic post and was later equipped with the most sophisticated weapons of the day. In 1893 the fort's Battery Potter…oh, a battery's a gun emplacement or artillery unit… anyway, Battery Potter featured the nation's first and only steam-lift gun battery and two 12-inch guns that fired half-ton projectiles for a range of seven miles. Of course, over the years a wide variety of weapons have been employed from the more modern canons to Nike Missiles during the Cold War. They are working on restoring the battery, now."

Emily was fascinated but she didn't particularly like talk of guns or artillery units, especially with Derek in Afghanistan. "What about these big houses? she wondered aloud. "When were they build and who lived in them"?

"Okay," John continued, "History House is one of 18 buildings along Officer's Row." His hand gestured towards the bay. "That's the name of the street that runs along in front of the houses. You came in the back door. Anyway, architecturally these structures are the most outstanding buildings on Fort Hancock and are unusual for officers' housing. They face away from the parade ground."

"I guess they liked the view of the bay," Emily offered.

"Ah, yes, you're right," John glanced at her and nodded. "The scenic view. So, anyway, the United States Army was very small in the 1890s and officers commanded great respect and, unlike today, each married officer was assigned his own house. So this one would have had lieutenants as well as captains living here. And their families," he added. "House number 12 is, well…*was* the most elaborate and expensive to build. It was the Commanding Officer's Quarters and a post of this size was usually commanded by a colonel."

"Are these house all alike?" Emily gazed at the hallway outside the office. She was anxious to see the rest of this fascinating old home."

"Well," John went on, "all the houses share the same exterior design. I mean they all reflect the formal Victorian-Era style of military living in the later half of the 19th century and they all face the bay; but there are three different floor plans due to the cost of building each house."

Emily thought about her own little house in Atlantic Highlands and how much their mortgage was each month. "And how much did they all cost?"

John tapped his pencil on the top of his desk. " Lieutenant's quarters cost around eight thousand dollars each, captains twelve thousand and the Commanding Officer's quarters cost a whopping nineteen thousand."

"Lord," Emily sat back and John laughed at the look on her face.

"So, he concluded, "History House is being restored and decorated to portray life in the army during World War two. It's a part of what we're trying to do to make Fort Hancock an interesting tourist destination. Oh by the way," he added," the National Park Service manages History House, but I'm looking for someone to be here this summer; and that's why you're here."

John pulled a white handkerchief from his uniform pocket and carefully blew his nose, returned it to his pocket, pulled her résumé in front of him and started reading, glasses propped on the end of his nose. He gave her a glance, hid a satisfied smile and thought to himself: pretty, prim and educated. She's perfect. When he'd finished he smiled again, tore a small piece of paper from a pad and carefully wrote a number on it, pushed that and the employee forms to her side of the desk and handed her a pen. "If you agree to the amount I've offered, fill these out and I'll show you around the house, give you an idea of your responsibilities."

Emily glanced at the slip of paper and was delighted. "I have the job? You're hiring me? This is *it*? How nice, um…I can't tell you how delighted I am to…um…Yes, this is fine."

"Yes, yes," he interrupted her, "I want you to start next Tuesday, Monday is your day off …let's see… May Fifth, The job will last until the first week of September. Oh, and of course we have special events that we would want you to cover, hmm, one in October and then the History House Christmas Party." He peered nearsightedly at his calendar. "The renovations will be complete by Monday. Yes! All finished. Uh, this will be your office." He looked around with interest as if seeing it for the first time, flicked a speck of dust off the corner of the desk. "I'd advise you to lock your belongings in the file cabinet when you're showing visitors through or while you're out of the office. At least lock the office door. No telling who may come in…uh…you know…" He swung the chair around until he was looking out the window. "OK, now, fill 're in."

Emily picked up the pen and glanced at the forms in front of her, wondering at the ease of this interview, happy that she was now gainfully employed again, even if it was only for the summer. Yippee, she thought to herself as she signed her name. I have a job! Wait till I tell Derek. I wish everything were as easy as this.

The first walk through the officer's house was another trip back in time. John led Emily into a bright kitchen, papered in a cheerful design of cherries and baskets of ivy on a white background. Starched curtains hung on three windows: two facing the open field, one facing north. An aging white sink sat under the window, next to the sink a squat icebox, topped by a fat, round engine that hummed quietly. A white enamel kitchen table with black trim, set with four white chairs and a baby's highchair, sat under the east-facing window. On one wall was a clock, its hands pointing to 5:30, and a 1945 Coca-Cola calendar with a shapely blond woman in a red-white-and-blue one-piece swimsuit, smiling and holding up a bottle of Coke, one toe pointed provocatively toward a beach ball.

Emily looked around with interest as John led her through a bright pantry and into a large dining room. The dining room was dark: dark wallpaper, dark curtains, dark furniture. A big table took up the center of the room. Six chairs were pulled up to the table, a sideboard filled one wall. A big window faced north and two west.

Both the dining room and the adjacent living room faced the bay at the front of the house and the wide veranda ran in front of both rooms. The front door was located between the two rooms and led onto the veranda. The living room was furnished with a couch, two chairs and side tables with lamps. A stone fireplace took up part of the wall opposite the window that faced the bay. Another two windows looked south and Emily could see the big brick house next door. Silver radiators sat beneath the windows in both front rooms. Candleholders with white glass tops sat on the mantelpiece, and next to the fireplace sat a straw basket with yellow silk flowers.

"Wow," Emily said out loud, "this is an amazing house. I've never seen anything like it." She gazed out one of the front windows at the seawall and bay, water stretching all the way to the mainland.

"You ain't seen nothin' yet. Three floors of big, big house." John let Emily gaze around, then pointed to an open door off the living room. "There's the *real* museum in this big, old house."

Emily glanced through the door from the living room and was suddenly overcome by a sense of uneasiness. The room was the officer's home office. It was furnished with a desk and wooden chair with wheels. An ancient black typewriter, complete with a half-finished letter, sat on a small table by the side of the desk. A large portrait of President Franklin Delano Roosevelt hung over the desk, a yellowed newspaper dated August 15, 1945, spread out on the top. The one window was dressed with brown drapes, and its window shade, like the one in the ranger's office, was pulled halfway down. John cleared his throat and waved importantly at the newspaper: "Of course, as the headline says, the end of World War Two was announced in the U.S. on August fifteenth."

Emily's eyes fell on an old, brown wooden radio against the wall and her apprehension increased. The room was closed to the public, a velvet rope looped across the door, but she stood for a long while gazing into the office. Suddenly a feeling of longing swept over her, a bead of sweat ran down her back and her breath caught in her throat. What in the world is wrong with me? She backed away from the door. "Is this the officer's home office?"

John watched her reaction, concerned, then sniffed, "Not home office, *officer's study*. They didn't have home offices then. You've got a lot to learn about World War Two." He turned away and she silently agreed and followed him back into the main hall.

CHAPTER TEN

BETTY

TEXAS 1939-1943

BETTY LEANED HER arm on the open car window and watched as the land flattened out and scrub oak, pine trees and sand took the place of the miles upon miles of forest and small towns they had passed on their way to Sandy Hook and the New Jersey coast. She searched the landscape for the first sight of ocean and breathed in the tangy salt air with pleasure.

At last, she murmured to herself, as close to home as I've been in so many years. And when they finally headed over the bridge from the mainland, tears pricked her eyes as the car seemed to float across the bay, water on both sides of the causeway as far as the eye could see.

When James had finished basic training in 1939, he was promoted to first lieutenant and sent to Fort Sam Houston in Texas and brought Betty and little James with him. The western states had been suffering through a long, bitter drought with such constant dust storms they were referred to as the "Dust Bowl." Texas was beginning to recover, but the years in San Antonio were hard for Betty. There never seemed to be an end to the dust that still seeped in through the window screens and under the door of the little stucco house James had rented for them. Little James was cranky with the heat, and the news from Europe was more serious with each passing day. Betty was homesick for the lavender mountains of North Carolina and would sob out loud as she washed the dishes or folded the laundry.

Fort Sam Houston was also home to General Roger Brooke Hospital, newly opened in November 1938, and Betty's daughter, Barbara Ann Warren, was born there during an early spring heat wave in May of 1940. Betty was enchanted with her baby daughter, her tiny hands and mop of dark hair. James was thrilled with his little girl and rocked her in his arms while Betty slept.

"Meet your new sister, Bobbie Warren," Betty told little James when they brought the baby home. She sat down on the couch and held the baby so little James could see her. "Bobbie, this is your big brother, James."

"Bobbie," he said, touching her curls lightly with his finger. "This is my own sister." Little James was timid, but he smiled then stroked her arm. "My very own sister."

Then on December 7, 1941, the Japanese bombed Pearl Harbor and America joined the war.

Fort Sam Houston was the largest army base in the country and was headquarters for the Southern Defense Command. It was slated to become a major internment center for prisoners of war, and James was promoted to first lieutenant and remained at Southern Defense. His fluent foreign languages and background in European history were mentioned. "At least I'm not going overseas," he consoled Betty, and she agreed. "As hot and dusty it is here," she told him as she dusted off the window screens in their bedroom, "I would be happy anywhere as long as I'm with you."

This time, Betty's mother didn't come to help her with the baby but she did call her on the phone, her voice familiar but far away on the long-distance lines. "Oh, my dear, I wish I could rush right down there to Texas and help you with the baby, but with the war coming so close…you know. I'll try to call you now and then and see if I can help. No matter how hard it is to get through now."

By the end of the summer, the dust seemed to be subsiding, and by November the weather had become almost pleasant, no dust cloud covering the sun. Betty would take little James and Bobbie outside in the backyard, and as James played in the dust she would rock Bobbie and sing:

Bobbie, Bobbie, pretty little girl, Mommy loves you so.
Bobbie, Bobbie, pretty little girl, Daddy loves you, too.
Bobbie, Bobbie, pretty little girl, Brother loves you more...

Little James would leave his toys and come and lean on her shoulder and pat his sister's dark curls.

In 1943, James was promoted to captain and received orders to Fort Hancock in New Jersey, where the Harbor Defense Control Post kept watch over New York Harbor and possible U-boat attacks on the city.

Again, Betty packed up their belongings for the long drive east by car, allowed by James' rank and position. "At least you'll be here in the United States," she declared firmly.

"And at least we don't have to go to New Jersey on a bus," James added, and danced her around the living room of their small stucco house in San Antonio.

CHAPTER ELEVEN

UPSTAIRS

APRIL 2009

JOHN BROUGHT EMILY upstairs to five rooms and a small bathroom. The master bedroom was on the southern end of the house and it was the first room they visited. Two windows looked out over the bay, two faced the house next door. There was a double bed with two matching dressers, a small chair with a fat pillow by one of the front windows, and a lady's vanity with a large mirror, small lightbulbs lining the top. A padded seat was drawn up in front. On top of the vanity: a woman's hairbrush, comb and hand mirror carefully positioned, a small, colorful dish filled with hairpins, a jar of Ponds skin cream, its label yellow with age and, oddly enough, a single glass candlestick. The vanity's skirt of pink-and-white flowered chintz ended in a ruffle. The seat was padded with the same flowered material; the windows were covered with soft, white curtains.

"The master bedroom," he said. "This is where the officer and his wife would sleep." Emily suddenly felt her face warm with embarrassment and looked away for a minute, then followed him through a large walk-through clothes closet and storage room into the second bedroom. This one was filled with toy cars and World War II airplanes; the walls were plastered with Captain America and Roy Rogers posters, the cot bed was covered in a brown-and-orange plaid coverlet and the windows were framed with matching curtains. A small dresser sat against one wall, books and crayons piled on top. A large toy truck sat by the closet door.

"I would wager a guess that this was a little boy's bedroom," Emily said, her composure restored as they were walking back into the hall.

John smiled and nodded to the next room. "Here's the little girl's."

The girl's room was furnished with a white bed with a pink coverlet, starched white curtains at the windows and a smaller edition of the vanity against one wall. A fabric-covered chair was pulled up to one of the windows and a number of dolls sat bolt upright in the chair, dressed in their 1940s styles. Emily agreed. "I'd say this is a little girl's room, pretty and dainty and just look at the dolls."

Next door was a sewing room, an old-fashioned black Singer sewing machine sitting against the far wall by the window. Next to the machine sat a small sewing cabinet with four little drawers for thread and needles and other sewing necessities. Against the sidewall, long bolts of material were stacked, a tall, brass wall lamp placed by the sewing machine. A stuffed headless mannequin stood in the shadows behind the rolls of fabric.

"During the war," John continued, "women spent many hours sewing clothes for themselves and their children." He paused and looked at the sewing machine, "just think of how it would be, pushing that pedal up and down for hours." He shook his head at the thought. "They also made linen and towels for the soldiers overseas and children made bandages for the Red Cross. Everyone pitched in."

Emily looked at the mannequin and frowned. What is *that*? She wondered but decided not to ask. She looked around the little room again. There were tan drapes on the one window and, again, the shade was drawn halfway down. Emily sneezed. "A little dusty," she said, "and definitely not my cup of tea," she added under her breath.

The final bedroom was next to the small bathroom. It was at the back of the house and overlooked the open field; it was furnished with a white crib and matching dresser, a rocking chair under the window and white curtains framing the view outside. The crib was filled with stuffed toy animals and a Raggedy Ann doll. Children's picture books were stacked on a small table and a dainty brush and comb were carefully placed on top of the dresser.

"Baby makes three," Emily said sadly as she stood by the door. Again she wondered, why her and not me, the thought that always haunted her when she saw women with their children…in stores, the laundry, the street…why? She mentally shook herself: in a World War II museum? That was really neurotic, Emily. No time or place for my regrets.

John pretended not to notice. "And next door is the bathroom," he said and led Emily out of the baby's room. "Nothing very interesting here," he added, "but everything works." A white tub with claw feet and a white sink took up one side of the room. A rather modern toilet shared a wall with a large linen closet. White-and-pink-checkered curtains hung at the windows, a fat bar of soap sat in a soap dish. A matching pink-and-white shower curtain on a curved rod was pulled back to show the old brass-and-silver showerhead. Over the sink a white, mirrored medicine cabinet reminded Emily of the old camp where she had spent summers in North Carolina.

"It reminds me of vacations when I was a kid," she said shyly. "We had a little bungalow in the Smokey Mountains and the medicine cabinet looked just like this one.'

"And some of the cabins in the national parks have them to this day," John added. He tapped his finger on the clear glass knob and seemed to be lost in thought.

As they headed back to the first floor, he waved his hand at the stairs that led to the third floor. "Nobody goes up there, Ms. Emily. Just two big rooms and, I believe, a shut-down bathroom. Nope, nothing up there at all, just junk." He kept up a running conversation: "Of course you'll get to know your way around in no time flat! You'll do just fine, I know you will. You really *do* have a head on your shoulders, don't you? You'll have no problems at all!" Emily found herself hurriedly nodding her head "yes" or "no" as he rattled off his observations. Rounding the landing, he pointed to an open door in the wall, "Oh, yes, of course you won't have to race all the way upstairs if you need to use the…uh…powder room."

Emily followed him and peered through the door. A small, tidy bathroom, complete with sink and toilet, was tucked away under the stairs. It was papered in a smart green-and-white print; green hand towels hung on a white towel rack by the sink. Crisp cotton curtains were hanging over a frosted window in the wall. "This is very cozy," she said as she looked around.

"And, of course," John hurriedly added, "it's for the guests, as well. Whenever they need the loooo, tooooo. Ha-ha!"

Emily thought: What in the world is that about? She raised her eyebrows and covered her lips with her fingers. "Yes, of course for the guests, too."

As they walked back to the office, Emily stopped to look at the photographs on the wall beside the kitchen: five framed black-and-white prints, all of them of army officers' wives from various eras. In one, a number of women in full skirts, wearing hats and gloves, stood on the veranda of one of the officers' houses. This one? Emily wondered.

In another photo a group of women were sitting at a dining room table, all turned in their chairs and smiling at the camera. They were dressed in suits with long, straight skirts, their hair in updos and pageboy bobs with peekaboo bangs. One of the older women, hair swirled on top of her head and a pouty mouth, was pouring tea into small teacups. "Oh, boy," Emily said, "what a crew, just look at that hair."

John stopped and glanced at the photograph. "Ah, yes, those are some of the ladies who lived here in Fort Hancock during World War II"

Below the updos and tea, a small photo caught Emily's eye. It was another black-and-white photograph: a young woman sitting on the veranda of one of the officers' houses with her children. The little boy looked around six and was leaning against the railing. His sister was a sturdy little girl and was sitting next to her mother; a baby girl in a sundress and sunbonnet, sitting on the woman's lap. The young mother was dressed in a sundress and was smiling, her pretty face glowing, happy. Emily bit her lip hard and turned her attention to the blackboard next to the photographs. Except for the date *August 15th* scrawled in white chalk, it was blank. Emily caught up with John as he headed for the office. "What's this date?" she asked, curious. The ranger glanced back over his shoulder and shrugged.

"I have no idea," he stopped and scratched his head, puzzled. "I don't even remember seeing that before. Well, sometimes the guests like to leave little messages. We have a guest book in the living room, but no telling what some folks will do when set loose in an old house. You'll see, you'll see. Now let's close this deal," and with that he disappeared into his office with Emily close on his heels.

Later, John walked Emily to her car and patted her shoulder. "Welcome to Fort Hancock, Ms. Craig," he said as he held the car door for her. "I'm sure you'll do just fine in History House."

"I'm excited," Emily nodded her head enthusiastically, "I feel like I'll fit right in, like it's a real home or something."

John waved and gave her a thumbs-up as she pulled out but after her car turned the corner and disappeared from view, he shook his head and shivered. "I do hope she'll be okay out here." He looked back at the officer's house, a small frown on his chubby face.

Emily called Jena and Ruthie that night, "Am I dumb to be so excited," she asked. It's just a summer job, you know, and not in publishing but it sounds like it will be a hoot!"

"Sounds like a hoot to me," said Ruthie, "and it'll pay the bills. Hey, I hope you can still come to Yoga."

Jena was fascinated. "Whoa, now *that* sounds like fun; more fun than cutting hair, anyway. Good going, Em."

Emily couldn't wait to tell Derek about her new job on the strange, isolated army base. When his face appeared on her computer screen, she told him about her interview, the strange old house on Sandy Hook. "And so, I landed the job without any trouble at all and I start on Tuesday and it lasts all summer. I didn't want to tell you about it until I knew for sure, but now I can. Yippee! It's pretty isolated out there but really, really interesting with rows of old barracks and old-fashioned brick buildings, right on the water. Wow! You wouldn't believe it!" Emily was excited for the first time in a long while.

"Good for you, Honey." Derek started laughing. "Don't get scared, though. From what I understand, it's supposed to be haunted."

Emily was shocked. "What? You mean a ghost?" Her imagination jumped into overdrive: *A soldier, dragging his rifle behind him, limped down the stairs and headed to the…Wait!…the officer's study…*"Oh damn, Derek, I don't want to hear this!"

Derek smiled at her expression. "One of those 'famous' ghost stories. They say a young woman walks the halls of twenty-four Officers' Row, crying. She often turns on a lamp in one of the upstairs bedrooms and stands looking out of the window. Nobody has ever said who she is supposed to be or why she is in that house, but there it is: a haunted house, right on Sandy Hook."

"Humph," Emily grumped. "Really nice of you to tell me this, Derek. But, no, I'm not scared and it doesn't seem haunted to me. Just isolated and old, old, old! But awesome, too. Now, tell me about *you!*"

Derek's unit had been sent to the army base near an ancient site: Baba Wali's shrine, a meditation chamber attributed to a saint named Baba Hasan, Baba Wali Quandary in local folklore.

"I'm just spellbound with this strange country, it's so totally wild with these wide-open plains and rugged mountains. Listen to this," Derek enthused, "excavations of prehistoric sites by archeologists suggest that this ancient area around Kandahar is one of the oldest human settlements known by man. What do you think about that?"

Emily didn't know what she thought about "that" but she did know what she was *really* interested in. "Is it dangerous, Derek?" she rested her chin on one hand, leaned closer to the screen, searching his face.

Derek hemmed and hawed a bit. "Well...uh...we *did* hear that last June some thousand or so inmates escaped from the local detention center after a Taliban attack. I guess that is kind of...uh, dangerous. Things seem pretty calm right now, so the prisoners must have disappeared into the mountains."

"Disappeared? Disappeared into the mountains? Are you kidding? Derek! What if they're still there, nearby?"

He ignored her questions. "It's pretty dusty here and mega dry." He smiled his wide, familiar smile and Emily found it hard to believe that he was so far away. She touched his Macintosh face gently with her fingers, smiled back and thought: Oh, dear, this is going to be a long year. She sat forward and kissed his image.

When they had signed off, Emily brought a load of laundry down to the washing machine and poured detergent in, closing the top with a bang. "Ghost, no way," she assured herself loudly and pushed the button, sending the washer rumbling into action.

She dusted around the living room before making a sandwich and a cup of tea and pulling a chair up to the little kitchen table. Leaning back in the chair, she glanced around the house and felt a small glow of pleasure: her bright kitchen and cozy front room, the big backyard, new spring growth. In the background a stern voice on the little radio droned: *Since the nineteen-seventies, thirty percent of adults and children have become obese. Computers and fast food have certainly contributed.* She smiled, feeling better after talking to Derek, and murmured, "You think?"

The day had turned out to be warm and sunny, a harbinger of better days to come, and Emily had opened the downstairs windows first thing that morning. Now, a slight breeze gently moved the kitchen curtains back and forth and she could smell spring as it floated in on the breeze.

"Things are going to be just fine," she said as she popped the last bite of her sandwich into her mouth. "I'll be fine, the new job will be fine and Derek will come home safe and *we'll* be fine." She washed the dishes and put them away, brushed the crumbs off the table into her hand and tossed them into the trash, then dashed upstairs, singing: *What's in my closet to wear on my first day of work. What oh, what oh, what ooh?*

CHAPTER TWELVE

BETTY

FORT HANCOCK 1943-1945

BETTY BLOTTED HER lips with a toilet tissue. She sat back on the vanity seat and looked at herself in the mirror: dark hair in a pageboy, shiny and black as a blackbird's wing, framed her pretty face, short bangs in front. Large dark eyes fringed with thick lashes looked back at her. Not bad, she murmured and smiled at her reflection. "Not bad for a thirty-year-old wife and mother of two. Yes siree, Bob, as Mr. Burrows would say."

The house was quiet now. Little James and Bobbie were playing in the toy room that overlooked an open field and the parade ground. Earlier, a staff car had pulled up by the back door and her husband had kissed her hard before he'd slammed out the screen door.

James always looks so handsome, she thought, and touched her lips with her fingers: tall and slim in his uniform with its silver captains' bars and his polished shoes. Gee, I really love this man. She smoothed her hair back, then stopped, a small frown on her face. What do I do if they send him overseas? How can I live my life wondering if he's in danger in Italy or France or some God-forsaken place in the South Pacific? How long can he stay here on Fort Hancock? How long before he's sent away?

She slipped off the seat and smoothed her red-and-white sundress over her hips, thinking about the day ahead. Once the dishes were done and the rooms dusted, she'd take the children to the Army Children's Center for the day. That afternoon, she had to attend an Officers' Wives' Tea at the Beck household; until then, Betty was free to walk along the shore, enjoying the salty ocean air.

When she thought about the war, when it felt like a heavy stone in her stomach, Betty would leave Fort Hancock and wander along the sand. Outside the gates, she was able to forget the reality of the bombing, the victims wild with fear, the terror on the other side of the world. For a while she could imagine a life without "The War," could think about life in Asheville. Back at Fort Hancock, the anxiety would start to tug at her again. The war is like a sullen stranger living in my home, she thought, her face sad.

Each evening her husband ate dinner, kissed her forehead and then closed himself in his study. She would hear the sober drumbeat of war news through the study door and the heavy feeling would fill her again.

However, Betty liked her big house, her life on Fort Hancock, and was happy with James and little James and Bobbie. She liked the sunny kitchen: its new stove, the icebox that hummed quietly in the corner. She loved the pantry with its glass-door cupboards filled with boxes and cans and containers, her new china and drinking glasses sitting on the top shelf. She liked the big, wide drawers under the pantry countertops.

Soon after they'd moved in, she'd ironed all her linen and stored it carefully in the drawers, where it was handy for entertaining the other officers and their wives. She was thrilled with the dining room and living room with their big windows that overlooked the bay. Sometimes, after she'd taken the children to the Army Children's Center, she'd walk through the rooms running a dust cloth over the pretty furniture, whisking the feather duster over the mantelpiece, admiring her home. She especially loved the wide veranda that stretched the length of the house. One warm Saturday afternoon James had dragged the porch chairs and table out and had attached the wooden swing to its metal rings overhead.

From the veranda, Betty could see the bay that stretched across to the mainland. When the weather was calm, the water was as smooth as glass, quiet, and when storms came in from the west the water would turn dull gray and toss waves against the seawall. Betty was intrigued, no matter what the bay offered; she enjoyed sitting on the steps daydreaming and looking out over the water.

As much as she loved her home, Betty wasn't crazy about the woman who lived in the house next door and she always glanced across the side yard before she came out to the veranda. Della was a high-strung woman, red hair worn in an intricate updo and small, bright eyes. She was married to an intelligence officer, a thin, angry man who seemed to take pleasure in scaring the wits out of his wife. Della had two grown children who were married and had homes of their own, so she spent most of her time gazing out her living-room window, hoping to corral someone with whom she could share her terrifying stories. Betty had heard a rumor that Della's husband was due to be transferred, and one night after James came home she approached him. "Is it true that Della's husband is transferring to Washington, D.C.?" She wiped her hands on a dishtowel.

James was sitting in the living room looking over the evening *New Jersey Mirror.* "Don't count on it, Honey," he said and turned the page.

"Aw, darn!" Betty said.

"What's up, Baby?" James glanced up and smiled. After all these years and two kids, he thought, I still love her so, want to pull her down in my lap and smooth that dark hair back from her face. He shifted in his chair and rustled the newspaper.

"Oh, nothing, really." Betty folded the dishtowel over one wrist and went back to the kitchen.

So now and then Della would still catch Betty, regale her with another "rumor" that had been confided to her "in strictest confidence." Standing by the kitchen window, Betty recalled an incident that had happened just after they first moved to the Fort Hancock house, in the spring of 1943. She had been hanging the wash on the line; Della had called to her from next door. In hushed tones she'd said, "An enemy submarine was spotted in the Connecticut River last night. It went right up the river as far as Middletown, then disappeared. What do you think of that?"

Betty was horrified. "That's terrible. I worry for us, for our children, you know? All the time now."

Her small eyes gleaming, Della continued, "Some people told my husband that spies landed on the banks in Middletown and are now hiding somewhere near Hartford. Sometimes," she continued, "I've heard that enemy U-boats are patrolling off the shore, right here at Sandy Hook. You can see the periscopes sticking out of the water." They were standing facing the bay, and both women glanced nervously at the water. Della gave Betty a tight little smile and swooped in again, "You never can tell, you know, you *never* can tell."

Betty was frightened, but she didn't want to bother James with this gossip and rumor; he seemed to worry about the war so much as it was, what with the war news night after night. As much as it made her anxious and unhappy, she tried to hide this from her husband. But as much as she tried, he noticed.

CHAPTER THIRTEEN

WOMAN ON THE SEAWALL

MAY 2009

THE FOLLOWING TUESDAY Emily started her new job. John had told her to wear neat but comfortable clothes and low shoes. "You'll be taking people up and down stairs and you want to be comfortable…you know, no jeans or sloppy stuff, but… well, you know." She put on a pair of stylish gray slacks, a black turtleneck sweater, brushed her hair hard until it shone and slid her feet into a pair of black flats.

Hmm, maybe the low shoes are for running away from a ghost, she wondered and smiled, dusted her face with the powder puff, rubbed a light pink lip balm on her lips. Before she left the bedroom, she stood in front of the full-length mirror and twisted from one side to the other admiring her reflection, the first time in a long time.

A quick cup of coffee, a bran muffin and she was anxious to go. She packed some personal belongings in a Pathmark green-bag, wrapping the desk items in an old newspaper whose headline screamed, *Senate Angrily Discusses Health Care for Second Day*, and Emily thought: Well, isn't Washington always angry now?

As she backed out of the driveway, her heart beat fast with excitement. At last she could put the savings back and pay the bills instead of piling them on the table, worrying about them day in and day out. Enough to tide us over. The spring day was sweet with blossoms beginning to touch the trees along the road out of town; masses of forsythia lined the highway. She turned onto Route 36 and headed towards the ocean and as she neared the Highlands Bridge she saw people had parked by the side of their summer homes, throwing open the windows and hanging the linen in the fresh air. The water in the bay was reflecting the early morning sun as she drove over the bridge.

The trip up Hartshorne Drive was as easy as it had been the week before, few cars going either way. At some of the hot dog stands, men stood on ladders getting their businesses ready for the summer ahead; along the roadway, town workers mowed the overgrown grass. Fun to watch this beach community come alive, Emily thought as she headed toward Fort Hancock. She liked the early spring emptiness of the beach town, the gradual awakening, but truly loved the hot summer days when people swarmed along the roads and shorelines. Until now, she hadn't realized how much she'd missed living near the ocean.

She tucked a silver curl behind her ear, turned the radio to a local station to catch up on the news and weather, humming along with the jingle that introduced the weather forecast: *Nice day...spring is here...summer is right around the corner...* And when the yellow barracks came into view, she stopped the car for a minute and peered at the old buildings, a small smile touching her lips, then continued on, looking forward to her first view of the big houses on the bay.

John was waiting for her by his green pickup truck and gave her a little salute as she climbed out of Derek's Honda and joined him. "Well, your first day, right on time and rar'n to go, huh, Ms. Emily?" They strolled across the lawn and climbed the back steps. He unlocked the door and handed her the keys. "The keys to your kingdom, Madam. Now it's all yours." He wiggled his eyebrows.

Emily thought: John, you're a very funny man!

He had cleaned out his office and Emily looked around with renewed interest. By the end of this day, this will be *my* office, my very own office. She rummaged around in the large shopping bag for the framed wedding photograph she had hurriedly wrapped in yesterday's news (*Senate Angrily Discusses Health Care for Second Day)* and set it on the edge of the desk. Nice, very nice, she thought as she dropped the shopping bag on the floor and shrugged out of her jacket.

"You can hang that behind the door," John said and pointed to a hook on the back of the office door. "Now, as I said, don't, and I repeat, *don't* leave your bag on your desk when you leave the office. You just never know who comes in…or out…"

Emily glanced at him. "I talked to my husband on Saturday. He told me that History House is haunted. Are you afraid a ghost will come and steal my pocketbook?" She smiled and hung up her jacket.

John snorted, "Yeah, if a ghost wears jeans and flip-flops. That old story's been around for ages. I think it's being revived to bring in the public, that's what *I* think, and, by the way, they never found any strange women in Missing Persons or anyone else for that matter, no calls, nothing. Just BS, that's all." He stopped, looked around for a minute, tapping his finger on the desktop. "Now, my phone number is here." The finger tapped a leather address book. "I have my office on the mainland but you can call me if you need anything." He looked around again. "Well, that's about it, yes…uh…well…hmm." He patted her on the shoulder and headed out the door.

Emily stood on the back steps and watched as he climbed into his green pickup and pulled away and thought, Wow! Then she turned around and started making herself at home in the little museum office.

By lunchtime she had cleaned out the desk drawers, straightened the books on top of the file cabinet, swished the feather duster around. The papers and forms were filed away and her familiar MacBook Pro was sitting on the desk in front of her. She sat back with satisfaction, twirled the feather duster around her little finger and thought: I'm starving! She'd thrown a peanut butter sandwich together the night before, decided to fix a cup of hot tea and sit in the bright kitchen to have her lunch. As she ate, she looked out at the open field and towards the parade ground. Did the officer's wife sit here in this very same chair and look at this very same parade ground? Suddenly energized, she began to imagine: *The officer's wife looked towards the parade ground as the troops marched by. "If only I could see my husband," the woman said sadly...* Enough of that wool gathering, Emily decided, hearing Auntie Emily in her head. Dusting the crumbs off her hands, she started cleaning up the remains of her lunch. The tidy kitchen lifted her spirit. As soon as everything was back in its place she took another walk through the house, spending a few minutes straightening out a chair here and a table there. Now and then she'd glance out one of the windows, looking for tourists. By the end of the day, she admitted it was still too cool and a few weeks early for any guests.

By five o'clock Emily was ready to close up and make the trip back down Hartshorne Drive and across the bridge. She locked the back door with satisfaction, my first day at work! She smiled to herself as she slid into the Honda and headed off Fort Hancock and back down Hartshorne Drive, thinking, Hot dog!

That evening, Emily was anxious for yoga to end so she could tell Jena and Ruthie about her first day. It seemed the class would never end. Once, Ruthie looked over at her and raised an eyebrow: "What?"

Emily began to think: exhaustion! Every muscle in her body was starting to complain and then, yoga was done for the night.

Adalet's Apron was practically empty when they settled down with their tea and sweet rolls and Emily had a chance to give both friends a detailed description of her first day at the old officer's house. "Guys, it may not be publishing, but it's really neat! My office is teeny weenie, but the rest of the house is huge: big high ceilings, windows in the front rooms that reach from the floor to the ceiling, and you should see the *veranda*. All the rooms are furnished in old-fashioned stuff from the nineteen-forties, I mean really old-fashioned." She stirred a little sugar into her tea, tasted it, put the spoon down.

Jena and Ruthie listened, amused.

"I'm kinda my own boss. I get to sit in my office or roam around. When someone comes, when they finally do come, that is, I take them around, tell them some of the history of Fort Hancock and the officers' houses, oh, and did I tell you? Derek said it's haunted. Some woman walks the halls or something, all very M. Night Shyamalan, you know. Of course, John, the park ranger, says it's all hooey, a story, made up for publicity." She paused a minute, then went on. "He told me that people probably won't start coming till it warms up a bit, but I get paid anyway."

Jena winked at Ruthie, "Sounds like some kinda neat job to me, sitting around in an office all alone in an old house on a deserted army base."

Ruthie brushed crumbs off her lap and added, dryly, "Or roaming around a haunted house all day."

Emily snorted, "Nice friends you turned out to be. If you two treat this as a big joke, well, I won't tell you all the juicy stuff I find out about this place. And, at least it'll pay the bill for a while." They ended the conversation, laughing together as they finished their tea and sweets.

The second week of May a few visitors started to arrive at History House. Emily found a box of brochures and flyers that gave the background of Fort Hancock and the house. She spread them out on the kitchen table and brought the guest register into the kitchen as well. She decided to start their tour in the kitchen, ask them to fill out the register, get some information for future mailings.

She closed her office religiously and carefully locked the door before taking the tourists through the house; she found that she loved regaling people with stories about the fort and the house that she'd memorized from the flyers. If there were any adolescent visitors, she'd tell them about the mysterious woman who walked the halls at night. Of course, they always loved it and would beg her to tell them more about the haunted officer's house. "Any vampires or werewolves? Aliens from space?"

The same evening the first tourists had arrived, Emily heard footsteps walking across the hall overhead and then a faint dragging sound. She'd been busy putting the brochures away and thought, Oh, crap, some kid's been left behind. She headed up the stairs but the rooms were empty. Imagination, she told herself and hurried out to her car.

Other than that event, the first week the big old house was still and empty and Emily relaxed.

But it would happen again.

When John stopped by to drop off her paycheck. Emily stopped him in the hall outside her office. "Hey, d'ya know something I don't know? I hear noises from upstairs. It sounds like someone is walking across the hall, but when I get there, nobody's there. It's pretty spooky, to say the least."

The ranger's heart seemed to skip a beat but he chuckled and patted her shoulder again. "This is an old house, Emily. Its old wooden bones are creaking and groaning like any other elderly soul. The walls are just chatting with each other."

"Maybe I'm scaring myself," Emily admitted, but John quickly turned away so she wouldn't see the horrified look on his face.

By the end of the second week, Emily stopped listening, began to feel more at home, but every now and then there'd be the odd noise: a man walking across the upstairs hall, a woman tiptoeing into one of the rooms, furniture being moved. At first, she'd bolt up the stairs, her heart in her mouth, but after a few days she stopped bothering. No matter how fast she was, the rooms were always empty, silent, undisturbed. Emily began to think the old house was really eerie. Old wooden bones or not!

That evening as she was closing the house, Emily paused on the veranda to watch the sunset over the bay, dropped down on the top step to relax and let her mind drift at will, watching the waves ripple against the shore. Suddenly a young woman appeared from the back of the house. She walked across the lawn to the seawall and stood looking out over the bay, her face hidden by long dark hair tossed by the breeze. She was tall, slim, pretty, wearing a short-sleeved white camp shirt, rather full navy shorts that showed off long, tan legs, but she seemed oddly underdressed for the cool May evening. She stood as if frozen in place, not looking left or right, her hands hanging by her sides.

Emily gave a small wave, called a soft "hello," then changed her mind and sat very still. The stranger appeared oblivious to her surroundings, remote, unapproachable. After a few more minutes Emily stood and turned back to the door, wanting to avoid disturbing the stranger's privacy. The woman never turned to acknowledge her. Puzzled, Emily softly closed and locked the veranda door, picked up her bag and car keys, headed back across the causeway. She thought: OK, now who in the world was that? The ghost? Nah! Now I'm being silly.

CHAPTER FOURTEEN

EMILY AND REBECCA

MAY 2009

EMILY'S DAY OFF was Monday, and after she'd been working at History House for three weeks she called Rebecca and asked her to meet for lunch.

She pulled into Seabiscuit's parking lot, gathered her bag and cell phone and headed for the door. Rebecca was comfortably tucked into one of the big booths near a mural of three jockeys on horseback; a bridle and a set of light spurs hung on the wall right above her head. Emily laughed and slipped into the booth facing her friend. "Hey, Bec, you fit right in."

Rebecca glanced up from her menu, mystified. "Huh?"

"The bridle and spurs." Emily nodded at the wall with its equestrian decorations and Rebecca smiled. She'd been an avid rider for most of her life and had owned a large sorrel mare named Sorrel, which she'd spent most of her free time riding. After her fourth child, or was it the fifth, Emily wondered, Rebecca had had to sell her beloved Sorrel and attend to her growing family. Now, she enjoyed meeting at Seabiscuit, surrounded by saddles, bridles, spurs, bits: everything but sawdust on the floor.

Rebecca shook her head and looked back at her menu. "This is a chicken day," she announced, plopping the menu down in front of her. "My appetite doesn't seem to be affected at all by my…er…condition." She looked up as the waitress arrived with a basket of bread.

Emily scanned the menu. "And *I've* decided to treat myself to a good steak and a sweet potato. And how about a nice wine? My treat!"

"Wine sounds lovely, but I'll take a nice tonic with lime, your treat. Now, tell me all about your job. I'm all ears." Rebecca handed the menus to the waitress, smiled and settled back.

Over lunch, Emily filled Rebecca in: about how much fun she was having, her little office, the tourists, how she would give them brochures and show them around the house. "They're so funny, some of them, reminiscing about the 'good old days,' how things were really great back then! Gawking at things and wondering how in the world women were able to live like that. You gotta come out and see this place sometime, you'll get such a kick out of it. Nifty job, thanks to Jane Rider!"

She added milk to her coffee and Rebecca wondered about the "mysterious ghost" Derek had mentioned. "So, here's the big question: have you met any ethereal strangers yet? Any ghosts roaming around the house or peering through the window at you? Anyone walking through the walls?"

Emily sipped her coffee and thought for moment. "I haven't *seen* any ghosts, but you know what, Bec? I hear them. I hear footsteps upstairs when I'm downstairs. Then I hear footsteps downstairs when I'm upstairs but nobody's ever there. Oh, and weird sounds. What's that about?"

Rebecca raised her eyebrows and started to laugh. "Are you kidding? I mean, come on, Em, I was only kidding. That's only a myth…uh…isn't it?"

Emily sank back in her seat, lost in thought. She was suddenly annoyed with Rebecca for laughing at the footsteps she'd been hearing, making a joke out of it. "Well, of course it's a myth," she snapped. "John, the park ranger, told me it's the old beams creaking, said it was 'the walls talking to each other' so it doesn't bother me. At all." Her voice added a period to her statement.

Rebecca looked surprised at her friend's sharp tone and raised her eyebrows again. "Whoa, what's with you, Em? I wasn't making fun of you."

Emily immediately felt contrite. "I'm sorry, Becca, I didn't mean to jump on you. I guess I'm feeling a little sensitive. It's a new job. I want to make enough to pay the bills. It's only been three weeks so far."

The two women changed the subject and topped off their meal with chocolate ice cream, smothered with whipped cream and nuts. "Nothing like chocolate to help stress," Rebecca remarked as she wiped ice cream off her chin.

Emily and Rebecca gave each other an extra-long hug in the parking lot before parting, and Emily turned the Honda toward home. She was mystified by her reaction to Rebecca's laughter. After all, this was her best friend. She realized she was becoming resentful of people making jokes about History House. She turned to a music station, tried to relax. By the time she pulled into her driveway, she'd decided to steer clear of discussions of ghosts and footsteps. She dropped her car keys onto the front hall table and then remembered she'd planned to tell Rebecca about the strange woman on the seawall.

But by the time she had brushed her teeth and settled into bed, she realized that she never would.

Toward the end of May, Emily decided to explore the top floor of the big house. She'd been told it was closed to visitors, that nobody had touched any of the rooms since the last family had moved out in the 1970s, but there were so few tourists coming to History House she was restless…and curious. The stairs led up from just outside the master bedroom on the second floor, a velvet rope looped across the bottom stair. She stood looking up the stairs and decided to bring some dust cloths and cleaning spray with her. Rattling around in the kitchen closet, she found a red plastic bucket, a mop and an ample store of cleaning supplies that she had used on the first and second floors. She dropped dust cloths, the big feather duster, detergent, Windex and furniture polish into the bucket along with some paper towels she'd found in Derek's Honda.

Emily carried her armload up to the top floor, pausing for a few minutes at the landing. The stairs ended at a large central hall, and she dropped the bucket and mop and looked around with interest. Two big bedrooms led right and left off the hall, one to the front of the house, the other to the back. A round window was centered over the landing and a closed door at the back of the hall apparently led to the unused third-floor bathroom. She picked up the cleaning supplies and walked across the hall and into the room that faced the open field. The two big windows were dull with dirt, the floors dusty. Faded flowered wallpaper hung from the walls, some sections curling onto the floor like ancient sepia scrolls. An old radiator sat under the windows, silver paint turning to dust. Here and there spots of red rust showed through the silver. A small chair was shoved into a corner next to a closet door.

Emily set the bucket down again and sneezing, walked across the hall to the second room. It was a mirror image of the first: two dirty windows looked out over the bay, an identical rusty radiator sat beneath the windows, a few pieces of furniture were pushed against the walls. This room was papered with green-and-white striped paper, faded, peeling away from the wall. She made a slow turn around and decided to start cleaning this room, with its view of the bay.

Humming under her breath, she turned back to pick up the bucket and cleaning aids, then paused. There, *there*, just then, in the room behind her, the sound of a woman sighing, and as it faded away, a soft laugh.

Oh, now what, I'm hearing voices? Emily chided herself. To silence her runaway imagination, she walked back into the hall and said in a loud voice, "This is an announcement. My name is Emily Craig, and I'm going to clean these rooms. I don't care if that disturbs you. Just get used to it!" Then she set to work.

There were no more sounds that day.

CHAPTER FIFTEEN

DR. AND MRS. WILSON

1944

THE WAR DRAGGED on, and in the summer of 1944 Betty's parents decided to come north for a visit in July.

Betty gazed at her mother's letter and poured herself a cup of Postum coffee. She sat down at the kitchen table and carefully slit the fragile envelope, sliding out the delicate paper. The family had been at Fort Hancock for over a year and she missed her parents terribly. Her mother had only seen photos of Bobbie that James had taken with his Brownie camera but had never met her new granddaughter in person. Betty welcomed every letter and when she read they were suggesting a week's vacation in New Jersey that summer, she felt her heart jump.

She waited anxiously for James to come home and met him at the back door, stumbling over her words. "Mother and Daddy are planning a trip up north to visit us! They think it's been too long and now that pleasure driving is allowed again, they're saving their gas rations and want to grab the chance." Betty chattered on as she hung his coat on the coat tree in the front hall. James was delighted to see his wife smiling and excited again and enthusiastically agreed.

The next morning she wrote back:

March 12, 1944

Dear Mom and Daddy,

I'm so happy that you're coming to New Jersey this summer. We have a big house in Fort Hancock. There are two big bedrooms on the third floor and you can stay with us as long as you want. I miss you so much and can't wait to see you. It's been so long, you won't believe how big little James is now and you will finally get to meet Bobbie.

Your loving daughter,
Betty

Gas rationing begun in December 1942 wouldn't end until August 1945. Speed limits were 35 miles per hour for the duration of the war and, for a short time in 1943, rations had been reduced further, all pleasure driving outlawed. Because Betty's father was a doctor he was able to obtain more gas stamps. Now that pleasure driving was allowed again, he decided it was time for a visit to his only daughter. "Heaven only knows what will happen next," he told his wife. "It's time for us to gird our loins and make the trip up to New Jersey."

Betty's mother agreed. "A wonderful idea, Dear. I do miss Betty so much…so very, very much. Doesn't seem right to have her way off in New Jersey on some island or something…and James and the children, of course. Just think, we'll finally get to see Bobbie, that darling little girl!"

Dr. and Mrs. Wilson sat down to start planning and Betty's mother happily took paper and a pen out of the desk drawer to send their itinerary to her daughter.

Betty dropped her letter in the PX mailbox, hurried home and up to the guest rooms. There were two big bedrooms and a storeroom on the third floor. One of the bedrooms faced the bay, and she decided she would ready this one for her parents. She dragged a bucket of warm, sudsy water up the stairs, scrubbed the windows until they shone, brought up the carpet sweeper and cleaned the rugs from one end of the room to the other. She dusted and cleaned until the room was "clean as a whistle," as she told James that night at supper. "My parents will enjoy Sandy Hook. It reminds me of North Carolina and the beaches are lots of fun. I think they'll feel right at home."

James liked Betty's parents. He was pleased they were coming to visit, especially because it brought a smile to his wife's face. "You can go onto the mainland, too," he said. The family was sitting at the kitchen table eating the tomato soup Betty had prepared for supper. "There's a little store in the village across the bridge, a diner, too." He blew on a spoonful of soup, popped it into his mouth.

"Grampa and Gramma coming?" asked little James.

"Yes, Grampa and Gramma are coming to visit in July when it is very hot and you must be very polite," James told them sternly, then softened and smiled at the children.

Grampa and Gramma. Grampa and Gramma, sang Bobbie and bounced up and down in her seat in excitement.

Betty buttered a piece of white bread with oleomargarine and passed it to her daughter. "Settle down and eat your supper, Bobbie," she said gently and turned back to her soup. Outside, the trees threw shadows across the ground and the sun began to sink into the west.

The weeks dragged by while Betty and the children waited for her parents to arrive. When they walked to the Army Children's Center, little James would ask over and over, "Grampa and Gramma comin' today?"

And every day, Betty would tell him how many more days they had to wait. "When it is hot," she said, and then "one month" and finally, "really soon, any day now." The officer's house was filled with excitement, with plans being made, discarded, then made again.

The evening before her parents were due to arrive, Betty picked wild daisies, filled a glass vase with water and popped in the flowers. She carried them up to the third floor, flowers for the bedside table. Smiling, she stood back and admired the arrangement. "I can't wait," she said. Then she hurried back downstairs.

Betty was drying the last dish late the next morning when the front gate called. "I have guests for Captain and Mrs. Warren." The guard was laughing and Betty guessed her father had cracked a joke or two. "Tell them I'm on my way." She wiped her hands on the towel, tossed it in the laundry basket and untied her apron. *Boy, oh, boy, oh, boy!* she sang and dashed for the back door.

The day had turned hot and muggy. She hurried across the parade ground and ignored the wet spots under her arms and down the back of her dress as the humidity caught up with her. She didn't want her parents to sit in the heat for a second longer than necessary

Dr. and Mrs. Wilson were kindly and gregarious, with slow, honey-toned, southern drawls and Betty needn't have worried. They were sitting comfortably in their sedan, rumpled and hot, but happy to be in New Jersey after months of saving gas coupons and driving up the East Coast in the summer weather. Her father was engaging the guard in a conversation: the trip north, the Outer Banks, weather in North Carolina, gas coupons. Her mother was watching with amused interest. The guard was leaning his arms on the driver's side window and the doctor was enjoying the conversation.

"Sunny every single day. Yes siree, Bob!"

"Big storms over the coast sometimes? I mean big storms?"

"Oh, well, sometimes."

"Hurricanes? And there are hurricanes, I've heard tell."

"Well, sometimes."

"I think I'll stick with New Jersey."

Betty joined the guard and waved at her father, "I'm here to collect my parents and I guess we need some kind of paperwork?"

The guard smiled, filled out a form and handed her a Visitor's Pass, "here you go, folks."

Betty climbed into the back seat of her father's dusty DeSoto. "Daddy, Mom, I'm so thrilled to see you! Thanks so much for coming! Welcome! Hello, hello. And thank you, Sergeant."

"Welcome to New Jersey, Sir, Ma'am." The guard saluted, smiled, stepped back into the gatehouse.

Mrs. Wilson turned and hugged her daughter over the seat back. "It was a long, slow trip, but it sure is pretty out here and now that I see y'all…well, it was worth it!"

Betty's father chimed in. "Sort of looks like the Outer Banks to me." Jamming the car into first gear, they lurched through the gate. "Looks like an army base," he continued. "Like when I was in Double-u-Double-u-One. Look at those barracks, reminds me of the old days."

Betty patted her father on the shoulder, delighted to hear his reminiscing again. It seemed like years since she'd seen her parents and she had a sudden, sharp pang of homesickness: for her home on the North Carolina coast, the warm water and white sand, the neat white houses in Swansboro.

Betty's parents were impressed with the house at 24 Officers' Row and exclaimed over the formal dining room and living room. Dr. Wilson peeked into James' study. "Now this looks like a man works in here," he commented.

Betty laughed. "Oh, Daddy, of course a man works there. It's James's study! Do you think I work in there? Doing what… copying down recipes, typing up grocery lists? Silly Daddy. Now, let me show you to your room."

When they saw the third-floor guest room, both the Wilsons raved about the high ceiling, the neat wall covering, the view through the big windows. Betty's mother put her suitcase on the bed and turned to her daughter. "While you fix a quick lunch, dear, "I'll put our clothes away and freshen up. It's been a long, hot trip."

Betty backed out the door. "I'll call you when lunch is ready." She softly closed the door behind her and hurried back downstairs.

That afternoon, Dr. Wilson took a nap on the porch swing. The two women walked across Fort Hancock to pick up the children at the Center.

Mrs. Wilson glanced at her daughter. "This war is very frightening. We've had sightings of German U-boats off the coast; sometimes piles of discarded clothing have been found hidden under the bushes just off the beaches. In fact, someone saw a U.S. warship torpedoing a U-boat right off Topsail Beach. That's what I heard, anyway." She shook her head in dismay.

Betty sighed. "I heard about a U-boat in the Connecticut River. I try hard not to think about it and we shouldn't talk about it in front of little James and Bobbie; sometimes they have nightmares about submarines and bombs. It's hard to get them back to sleep."

Betty put her arm around her mother as they walked the rest of the way, talking quietly about the air raids and food rationing. When Little James and Bobbie saw their grandmother, the somber atmosphere quickly changed as the two children raced outside to meet them.

"Gramma, Gramma!" little James shouted. "We waited a million days for you to come!"

"Waited million days," parroted Bobbie. "Million, million, million!"

"My darlings!" Mrs. Wilson swept the two little ones into her arms and that was the end of the war talk.

Betty set the formal table in the dining room. She chose a white tablecloth from the pantry drawer and smoothed it over the table. Her mother helped set the places with the china and silverware Betty had been given as wedding gifts years before.

"I remember these dishes," Mrs. Wilson said dreamily. "Daddy and I went shopping in Raleigh and found these lovely dishes and silverware in Sears, set on a table, looking like it was ready for guests. We knew these were just right for you and James." She smiled at Betty. "I'm glad you're getting to use them."

Betty put out drinking glasses. "I use them for special occasions and this is a really special occasion." She thought: How I've missed them, my Mom and Daddy. Nothing is too good for them. She'd gone to Fort Hancock's commissary early in the morning and purchased cube steaks for dinner. Now, potatoes were boiling on the stove, rolls browned in the oven and while they waited, the women sat at the kitchen table, shelled fresh peas and tossed them into a glass bowl.

Betty looked up at her mother, an empty pea shell in her hand. "Tomorrow, James is lending his car to us for the day. This way you don't have to use your gas ration. Daddy can drive us over the causeway and we can visit the village on the other side of the bridge." She tossed the shell into the trash and picked up another pea. "He said there's a little store there and a diner where we can have lunch. We can spend the afternoon walking around the village seeing the sights."

Her mother was pleased. "How nice of James, Dear. He's a very special man, isn't he? We've always been fond of him, ever since he was a young fellow back in Swansboro High School. Daddy likes to visit with him so much now he's a grown man." Betty smiled at her mother and the two women sat shelling peas in a companionable silence. The pot of potatoes burbled gently on the stove.

Dinner was a success; everyone asked for a second helping of mashed potatoes, peas and rolls. Betty had baked an apple cobbler the day before and served it warm, with coffee from their special coffee ration. After dinner, she shooed the children onto the veranda to play while Betty and her mother cleared the table and washed the dishes. Dr. Wilson and James disappeared into the study and closed the door.

The sound of the nightly news began, a soft murmur through the door, and Betty glanced at her mother. "James does this every night after dinner. He listens to a man named Gabriel Heatter.

Isn't that a strange name? Like some kind of furnace. Anyway, Gabriel Heatter always says there's 'good news tonight,' but it scares me anyway. I never know what's happening out there and I'm afraid to ask James. I wonder if it's something awful, Mom. Do I even want to know?"

Her mother put her arm around her and gave her a hug. "It will be over someday, Honey, just like World War One, and then life will go back to normal, just like before. Daddy listens to Gabriel Heatter, too. He says he's a good newsman, seems to be something that the men want to do, you know? Be on top of it all. Maybe it is good news." She stroked a lock of her daughter's hair back from her face and behind her ear, the dishtowel forgotten in her other hand, and stared into space, then shook her head. "Enough of this war talk." She looked at Betty and smiled brightly. "Now…let's take the children for a walk on the seawall before they go up to bed."

CHAPTER SIXTEEN

THE THIRD FLOOR

MAY 2009

EMILY EMPTIED THE bucket of cleaning supplies, carried it back downstairs to the kitchen and stood at the sink. As the bucket slowly filled, she gazed out the window, watched as the groundskeeper mowed his way in sweeping circles around the grounds. On her way back upstairs, she grabbed the broom from the broom closet in the hall and her little transistor radio from her office.

She wanted to tackle the windows, turned to a soft rock station, unrolled paper towels and sloshed the warm soapy water across the glass, humming as the water ran brown and muddy down the windows. She unrolled more towels and started in with the Windex, rubbing until the first sunlight in years fell across the dirty floor and dust mites danced in the light.

She stepped back, wiped a hand across her forehead and grumbled. Damn, it's stuffy, hot as mid-August and it's only May. She swept the floor and pushed the dust into a pile next to the door. More dust danced in the sunlight and Emily pulled a tissue from her pocket and wiped her streaming eyes, thinking: Why did I ever start this?

This was the second day she'd been on the third floor: scrubbing, dusting, sweeping and pacing between the two bedrooms and now she stood looking out of the clean windows. How pretty

Sandy Bay looks with its little waves hitting the seawall, she thought. I wonder who stood here looking out of this window back in World War II. She sneezed again and turned back to her cleaning.

As the day wore on she filled the bucket and hauled it to the third floor over and over. After the fourth trip up and down the stairs, she glanced at the closed door in the central hallway and decided to check out the third-floor bath: please, please, please, let the water be turned on. She sneezed loudly, found the tissue again and took a swipe at her nose. John said he thought it was an old, unused bathroom but why didn't I bother to check it out myself, she wondered.

She crossed the hall and opened the door and was shocked to find a large storeroom filled with furniture: blond credenzas, antique bedside tables, glass-fronted cabinets and two 1960s-style twin beds pushed against one wall, boxes of books and three old living-room lamps stacked on top. Two framed Maxfield Parrish 1909 vintage prints leaned against one of the walls.

She stared. Wow, now this really *is* a find. Laughing out loud, she decided that each room should have a framed print, pulled them out of the storeroom and leaned them against the wall by the stairs. Although she was not thrilled with the lack of third-floor running water, she decided to pick her way through the storeroom when she had finished cleaning, find some pieces to furnish the bedrooms. What fun, she thought and closed the storeroom door.

By the end of the day, the first room was clean. The windows sparkled and the floor was scrubbed within an inch of its life. Emily found a small jar of white paste in the office and smoothed the wallpaper back on the wall, finished by placing the small chair by the window. She stopped and looked around the room. Without the years of dust and grime, it was a nice room with high ceilings and plenty of space. I wouldn't mind having a room like this, she said and sat in the little chair with her legs stretched out in front of her, fanning her face with the feather duster. A room with a view.

The afternoon sun was sinking as she carried the last pail of dirty water down the stairs and rinsed out the bucket, turning it upside down in the sink. She brushed her hair back from her face.

As Emily turned away from the sink, a sudden breath of air appeared on the third floor and moved a small piece of paper towel across the hall floor and disappeared.

CHAPTER SEVENTEEN

THE MAINLAND

1944

JAMES BACKED HIS car out of the garage and parked it by the back door. He handed the keys to Betty's father and headed for his office building. Dr. Wilson slid into the front seat with the *Daily Clarion Tribune* and lit a cigar. Betty and her mother gathered the children for the walk across Fort Hancock to the Children's Center and waved away her father's offer of a ride. He sat back with a satisfied grunt to wait for the two women, lit his cigar and opened the paper to the world news.

"It's too nice a day to waste it all in a car." Betty said and watched little James and Bobbie as they dashed across the grounds. "I like this walk in the morning. It does my heart good to see the children so full of life."

The women walked arm in arm as they crossed Fort Hancock chatting about the children and the cost of food. Up ahead the Service Center building stood on its patch of grass, children lining up by the front door, boys in one line and girls in another. Betty and her mother joined the group of women standing by the front porch. They all watched the lines move their children through the doors into another day of summer play, freeing them to spend hours shopping or taking tea with the other army wives.

"Humph," Mrs. Wilson said under her breath. "Not that I begrudge anyone an afternoon off, and far be it from me not to welcome our day together, but I must say, Betty, when you were a child, *I* was the one who took care of you." She smiled thinly at the woman standing next to her and turned back to her daughter. "No child centers for you, oh, no! If I went shopping, you went with me. If I visited with my neighbors, you played with their children while we visited. That's the way it was back then." She shook her head, furrowed her brow. "I guess I really don't understand this younger generation."

Betty laughed. "Come on, Mom. I remember Sally Anderson staying with me now and then, and she was only twelve years old, for Pete's sake!" The last of the boys and girls disappeared through the door and Betty and her mother turned away.

When he saw the women, Dr. Wilson tossed out his cigar, folded up the *Tribune* and tucked it down the side of the seat. Betty jumped into the back and leaned her arms on the front seat as her father started the car, cranked it into gear and headed toward the front gate. It was a beautiful summer day and both Betty and her mother wore light, pastel dresses and open-toed sandals. Dr. Wilson drove carefully down Hartshorne Drive and Betty looked out the window, thinking about the day James had first brought her and the children to Fort Hancock. "It seems like a hundred years have passed since we first arrived," she said softly. "Here I am, looking out the window at the same bay, the same ocean."

Mrs. Wilson smiled, "Time flies when you're having fun. My, my, just look at those waves. Almost as big as the ones in North Carolina."

"Makes me homesick," Betty murmured.

Dr. Wilson shifted the gears again. "Do y'all see any enemy subs?" They laughed nervously. "Ha, I really don't believe that hogwash. I think it's all propaganda to keep us in line." Betty looked at her mother and rolled her eyes.

The little village on the mainland was small and quaint, with houses lined up neatly on either side of the main street.

The store was in the middle of town, filled with wonderful items: knickknacks, beachwear, sodas, homemade pies and Drake's Coffee Cakes in cellophane wrap. Betty and her parents wandered around looking at what was on offer. Near the back door a familiar red icebox kept the sodas cold, terrycloth towels and beach wraps hung from hooks on the wall, pies were lined up on the front counter under waxed paper and another case was filled with china statues of mermaids and colorful fish, small boxes of saltwater taffy and a group of shells. A rack next to the front door was filled with comic books and magazines. A small, elderly woman sat behind the counter, knitting; the soft clicking of the knitting needles followed them through the store.

Betty's mother turned from the case. "Miss," she paused, considered the woman's age, shrugged. "I'd love to buy some of these shells, and certainly one of your delicious pies. We'd like to have lunch and walk around a bit. May we buy these now and come back later to collect them?"

The woman stood, stretched stiffly and put her knitting on the seat of her chair. "Of course, and by the way, there's a small fair just outside of town. Maybe you'd like to see that, too. We really enjoy our summer fairs and we welcome all strangers."

Betty and her parents piled into the car and headed out of the village. Betty leaned her arms on the back of the front seat again and looked through the windshield. She could see the fair in the distance: a tall Ferris wheel turning slowly, colorful flags, a number of white circus tents with lights strung between them and, here and there, wooden booths. Betty was enchanted. "Oh, I wish we'd brought the children. What an exciting surprise."

The family wandered around looking at the sights. "Reminds me of the old days," said Dr. Wilson. "Big state fair down by Raleigh. Had cattle and sheep, even pigs. Lotsa carnival rides, the 4-H tent with cooking and sewing contests."

"I won an award for the best flower arrangement one year." Mrs. Wilson gazed into the distance. "Don't you remember, Daddy?"

Betty and her father threw hoops around a row of glass bottles and missed them all. They visited the Home and Garden tent and tasted samples of honey and home-made jelly on crackers. "Mmm, mmm, good." Mrs. Wilson bought them both a small bottle of honey.

Betty presented them with a small, clear glass dog filled with tiny candies. "It reminds me of the olden days. You used to buy me these when I was a little girl." She smiled at the memory.

When they finally drove away from the fair, Betty looked out the rear window. The lights from the fair sparkled behind them and on the side of a garage she saw the drawing of a funny little man with a big nose, the top of his bald head peeping over a wall and his fingers clutching the top with the words KILROY WAS HERE printed below. "This will be one of my 'wonderful days,'" she said dreamily. "I think I'll start a collection of 'Wonderful Days.'" They found a parking space in front of the small, silver diner on the edge of town. The Miss American Diner offered *"Good Food for Hungry Americans."*

Dr. Wilson held open the glass door and they trooped into a narrow room: booths along the outside wall by the windows, a counter with a red top and stools with matching red seats, blackout curtains tied back to let the sunlight in. Betty slid into one of the booths across from her mother, and her father excused himself for the "little boys' room."

The waitress brought water and menus for the table. "Today's special is hot dogs and baked beans. We also can make a hamburger if you want." She pulled a pencil from behind her ear and opened an order pad.

"Hot dogs and beans all around," ordered Dr. Wilson as he rejoined his family. "I think we're all pretty hungry by now, right, folks?"

Betty looked out the big window at the village. It was the first time she'd been on this side of the bridge and she was curious about the people who lived on the mainland. Were they frightened, too? Did they also look out at the bay, watching for periscopes in the water, spies hiding in the dark?

"Here you go, folks." The waitress arrived with a big, silver tray and put plates down in front of them: a grilled hot dog, a small mound of baked beans and a slice of fresh tomato on a lettuce leaf.

"As soon as we finish lunch we'll go back and collect our purchases at that little store," Mrs. Wilson said as she picked up her fork. "I love the honey, too. We can put it on toast in the morning. The children will love it."

Betty's father cut up his hot dog and spooned some beans into his mouth. "Very good, very good! Almost as good as North Carolina," he said and returned to his lunch.

Betty looked across the table at her parents and smiled. This is Mom and Daddy, my mother and father, here all the way from North Carolina. I'll always treasure this day. Then she returned to her hot dog and beans, the war forgotten for a brief, glorious moment.

CHAPTER EIGHTEEN

AN OLD PHOTOGRAPH

MAY 2009

THE SECOND ROOM was even dustier than the first. Emily hauled a bucket of water up the stairs the next morning and prepared herself for another day of dirt and grime.

The night before, she'd laughed out loud when she looked in the bathroom mirror: smudged with dirt, dirt caked around her eyes and dirt running down the front of her shirt. Good grief, if Derek could see me now! Scrubbing at her face she thought, Lucky I didn't shop for groceries on my way home. I would've scared the wits out of everyone.

By the end of the third day, she was finished with both rooms and stood back to admire her hard work. I like this, she thought as she mopped her face. Not that anyone will come up here, but I'm glad I cleaned these rooms. Of course, I can come up here myself when I want to hide out.

She stacked the mop, pail and cleaning aids next to the stairs and turned to the storeroom. The two bedrooms were clean, and Emily wanted to see what furniture she could find: a bed (with no mattress) for each bedroom, bedside tables, lamps, two cabinets and the big credenza. She ticked items off her fingers: the credenza can go in the front room, one of the cabinets in the back, then bed, bedside table, lamp and the Maxfield Parrish prints and that will complete both rooms. Yes, that will do quite nicely.

In the back of the storeroom, she saw a small desk pushed against the wall. She hoisted the boxes off the beds and dragged them into the hall, books spilling out across the floor. She was able to haul the beds out of the storeroom and shove them into the bedrooms. The bedside tables were light enough to carry out, and with a lamp centered on each, the rooms took on a lived-in look. She glanced at the desk, scratched her chin and decided that would be next instead of the cabinet and left the heavy credenza until last. Emily was covered with dust and pulled out a tissue to mop at her eyes again. I hope nobody shows up to visit History House today, she thought fleetingly, then laughed aloud.

After hauling and shoving more furniture and boxes around, she had the little desk out of the storeroom and into the back room, underneath one of the big windows. She hurried into the hall and found the furniture polish and a clean rag next to the bucket.

A quick spritz of polish and this little desk will look like new, she thought, and set to work. The desk was pretty, with two large drawers in the front and a row of small drawers at the back of the desktop. Emily rubbed the polish onto the wood and it took on the deep, rich tone of fine mahogany. She polished the smart brass handles until they shone, then sat back on her heels and ran her fingertips over the silky finish. What a pretty little desk, she thought. Did the officer's wife write letters here?

The two drawers in front were empty and free of dust, so a quick flick of the dust cloth was enough, but the little ones in the back were difficult to open. She carefully slid them out one at a time and cleaned each. The last little drawer wouldn't budge. She sat back again, then tugged at the brass knob, tried to pry open the drawer. Little by little the drawer inched out, then stuck fast. Damn. Emily glared at the desk. Damn, damn, damn!

She dashed downstairs, found the can of WD-40 spray under the sink and triumphantly raced back upstairs with it in her hand. A little squirt of oil and the drawer finally came loose. To her dismay, she saw that it had been locked. The tongue was now jammed back into the lock and the brass keyhole was twisted.

Rats, Emily thought, disgusted. Of course I would break something. Pulling the little drawer further out, she checked to see if there were some way she could repair the lock and thought: I broke it, now what do I do? How do I explain *this* little adventure to John?

Then she saw the photograph. It was stuck in the back of the drawer and was yellow with age. It showed a man and woman next to a 1930s-style coupe. The man was probably in his late 30s and was wearing an army uniform shirt over a pair of dark bathing trunks. He was tall with light hair cut short, a wide smile, a handsome face.

The woman was slim with dark hair in a pageboy and bangs. She was wearing a sundress and sandals and was sitting on the fender of the car smiling as a breeze ruffled her hair. Two children, a boy and a girl, maybe six and four, leaned against her leg, smiling gap-tooth smiles. The car was parked beside the beach, the ocean visible in the distance behind a grove of pine trees.

Emily stared at the photograph: I'll bet this was locked into the drawer sometime during the Second World War. She held it up to the light and studied it carefully, turned it one way and then the other and flipped it over. On the back was a small cartoon drawing of a bald man with a big nose peering over a wall, and the words *We were here* written in a sloping handwriting. She flipped it back and thought: Huh, that's an odd little picture; and a bell went off somewhere in the back of her mind. There was something familiar about the young woman and a strange longing washed over her: the same feeling she'd experienced the first time she'd glanced into the officer's study. She closed her eyes for a moment, shook her head, looked again, thought about the army officer and his wife together in the big bed downstairs, making love, and shivered.

What's the *matter* with me? She was mystified. Who does this woman remind me of? Why should some old photo make me so nostalgic and what else…envious?

She touched the children with a fingertip, again felt the loss of her own unborn babies. Why her and not me, she thought, and for the briefest moment, the soft laugh seemed to hang in the air. Brushing away her silly thoughts, Emily put the photograph back, closed the little desk drawer and hurried back downstairs, tossed out the dirty water and wrung out the mop. It was time to put everything away and close up for the night. But as the darkness started to move in from the ocean, as she headed for home, her mind kept returning to the photograph, over and over again.

No amount of Norah Jones would put Emily's mind at ease that night.

CHAPTER NINETEEN

A DAY AT THE BEACH

1944

ONE HOT SUMMER morning, about a month after Betty's parents had returned to North Carolina, James slammed through the back screen door, wandered into the kitchen and kissed Betty on the top of her head. The children were at the kitchen table with milk and toast and she had just made herself a cup of Postum coffee.

James made a face at the Postum, sat down at the table and began to twirl a spoon around with his finger. "How would you like to take a picnic to the beach on the south end of Sandy Hook?" He smiled at Betty's expression. "We can take the children along and some lunch and spend the day. Would you like that?"

Betty's eyes widened in surprise. James always rushed out the door in the morning, was hustled away in the army sedan and never returned until sundown. The war had made everyone worried and anxious, and the busy husbands stationed at Fort Hancock rarely had time to share lunch with their families. A picnic and a day at the beach? Unheard of!

"What's happened? Is everything all right?" Every surprise meant a moment of panic now, even a day at the beach.

"The building's being fumigated. Cockroaches, ugh," James continued, leaning back in his chair and holding his nose. "We have to spend the day away from our offices. I thought it would be fun to spend the day together…in the fresh air! I just can't spend this beautiful day at home in my dusty study. To heck with it…let's just go!"

Betty was delighted and the panic subsided. "Wow! I guess I have these awful bugs to thank. Yes! Yes, yes, what a welcome treat. I'll fix sandwiches and make some punch. We have a little fruit and some cake, too. I made it first thing this morning." The idea was delightful.

She hustled the children upstairs to change into their bathing suits and terry rompers, falling over each other on their way to their rooms. While they were changing, she hurried into her bedroom to dig out her own bathing suit and James' blue wool bathing trunks, stacking shirts and shorts on the floor as she searched. She wriggled herself into her suit and pulled a terrycloth robe over her head, ran a comb through her hair. Bobbie had put her suit on backward and little James had tossed his romper in a heap under the bed. "It looks like a girl's sunsuit and I'm a big boy," he sulked as Betty fished it out and forced his squirming body into the romper. Bobbie stood in the doorway with her thumb in her mouth.

"That's very silly, James. Look how good Bobbie is now that her suit is on the right way." She shook her head and then called to James as she herded the children back downstairs. He tossed the paper down and headed upstairs to take his turn changing.

Betty took out white bread and spread it with peanut butter and jelly and then wrapped the sandwiches and some cake in the waxed paper she saved under the sink. Humming, she washed and dried four small apples and put them into a cloth bag, filled a glass jar with fruit powder and water and shook it briskly. Everything was packed into a wicker basket and by the time James came back downstairs, the family was ready.

The children had found their beach pails and shovels and were waiting anxiously by the back door, wanting the day to begin before someone called and ordered the captain back to his office.

Gotta go now, now, now! Wanna go to the beach now... they sang while they waited.

James helped Betty carry everything out the back door and then backed his little car out of the garage. "Into the car, Eager Beavers," he called and the children clambered into the back seat, crowded in with the picnic basket and towels. Betty slid in next to James. It had been a long time since she had gone off Fort Hancock with her husband and it was a thrill when they drove past the saluting army police guards and down the post road to Hartshorne Drive.

The summer day was warm with a blue sky and a few wispy clouds along the horizon, the water calm in the bay. And as they turned onto the main parkway, Betty could see the ocean in the distance. Oh, God, she thought, I wonder if we will see any periscopes out there, then banished the thought from her mind. Instead, she sat with her elbow on the open window and watched as they drove past the groves of stunted pine trees and walls of gorse bushes. "I will love this day," she said out loud, "and I will remember it forever. This is another day for my 'Wonderful Days' collection."

James leaned over and opened the little glove compartment. "Here," he said, handing her the small, square camera. "We can take some pictures at the beach, some new photographs of the children before they grow up and get married and move away." He winked in the rearview mirror.

The children giggled and Betty smiled to herself. "Oh, yes, I will love this day," she told herself again. "Whatever is to come now, or next year or even the year after that, I will always remember this day and remember how much I loved it, how wonderful it was." Then she started to sing softly to herself.

The southern end of Sandy Hook was filled with picnic tables and ice cream stands. On the bay side of the road, a small group of tourist cabins stood among tall pine trees; children ran among the trees and played by the cabins' steps. People walked along the road in bathing suits and robes. Women with big straw hats dragged children along the sand.

James found a side road and followed it toward the ocean. "This looks like a good path down to the shore," he said, "and just look. There is the big, blue Atlantic Ocean."

The children bounced up and down in excitement singing: *Ocean, ocean, big blue ocean...!* He parked by a gorse bush and the family piled out of the car. James dug a blanket out of the trunk and helped Betty carry the towels and basket as the children raced onto the sand. Halfway down the beach, James spread the blanket out on the sand and plopped down. "Now, this is the life," he said and closed his eyes.

Betty walked slowly across the sand and joined the children at the edge of the water. Small waves were rolling back and forth and a lacework of foam washed up onto the sand. The children squatted down and started digging in the sand, filling their pails and chatting among themselves, their voices carrying on the breeze. Betty slipped into the ocean and sat down in the waves, let them wash over her and leaned back on her elbows, her head hanging back so the sun shone on her face, her hair just touching the water.

She thought: I don't care if an enemy submarine pulls up onto the beach and two hundred spies race into the gorse bushes. She swished her feet back and forth in the cool water. This is such a wonderful day, even *that* can't spoil my fun. Smiling at her nonsense, she lay down in the water and let it cover her body.

At noon, Betty called to the children and they joined James on the blanket. Little James opened the basket and passed the sandwiches around; Betty poured punch into tin cups. They shared the fruit and cake, sat on the blanket together eating and looking out to sea, enjoying the sun and the water and each other.

The sun moved across the sky. Betty stretched out next to James on the blanket and watched as the children ran in and out of the waves, then closed her eyes and drifted off. James' hand reached out and took hers, closing it in his own, his breath warm in her ear. When she opened them again, he was sitting next to little James and Bobbie as they pushed sand into a pile over his feet. The war seemed far away and oddly diminished.

At the end of the afternoon, she called the children back to the blanket, combed their wet hair and dried them with a towel. She combed her own hair with her fingers and slipped her sundress over her head. "Here, let me help you," James said, and smoothed her dress over her hips, one hand moving across her thigh. Together they gathered up the blanket and the basket, headed up the sand to their car, all of them dizzy with the sun and covered in sand.

James slipped on his shirt and loaded everything back into the car, then waved to a man walking back up the path. "Excuse me, Sir," he called, "would you please take a photograph of my family?" He handed him the Brownie and gathered Betty and the children around him. Betty laughed and shinnied up onto the car fender, the children resting against her leg. James leaned back against the side of the car and crossed his arms. "Smile like a big alligator, everyone!" Betty smiled, the children laughed and the stranger pushed the button: taking a photograph that would end up in a small desk drawer and, more than half a century later, change another woman's life.

CHAPTER TWENTY

EMILY FINDS A TREASURE

JUNE 2009

J UNE WAS A rainy month. Emily began to stop at the Coffee Bean on the way to Fort Hancock: a quick sprint from her car to the shop and then a dash back, balancing a large latte in her hand. The young counterman would have her coffee ready as she came sailing through the door, shaking the rain off her hair. The second week he started a daily banter, flirting with her as she paid for her coffee and she'd smile at the tall, gangly young man as she passed her money over the counter.

"Nice day, Pretty Lady," he'd say, leaning his elbows on the counter and winking at her. "You bring *sunshine* into my lonely, rainy and boring life."

Emily began to banter back, enjoying the innocent flirtation. "You make my day, too, Kiddo," she'd tell him before dashing back to her car. She would see him with his wide grin watching her through the glass window as she drove past. All the way out to Fort Hancock she'd sip her latte as the wipers drummed back and forth, the Honda passing cars that splashed big puddles onto the windshield. Soon the morning ritual became comfortable, fun; not a bad way to start the day.

The rain kept museum visitors away. Emily spent more time in her office pouring over the flyers and brochures she put out for the guests or wandering around the house. One especially wet afternoon she started going through one of the big drawers in the pantry. Among loose papers and envelopes she discovered an old bronze picture frame and more photographs, evidently stored away years before. She took the photographs back to her office and spread them out on her desk, studying them with interest. Fort Hancock dated back to just after the Civil War, but the photos looked no older than the turn of the twentieth century: pictures of the officers' houses lined up along the bay and looking smart, well cared for; more pictures of a large group of enlisted men from WWI standing on top of a huge cannon that faced out to sea; still more of the officers' wives dressed in their best go-to-meeting finery and, as always, sitting around somebody's dining room table smiling over their teacups.

My God, Emily thought as she shuffled through the stack, these women did nothing but go to tea parties. They must have spent half their lives in the ladies room. However, she had to admit she loved the old hairstyles and dresses and little veiled hats.

Looking at the photographs gave her an idea. Stuffing them back where she had found them, she raced up to the third-floor bedroom and pulled out the little desk drawer. Slipping her fingers into the back of the drawer, she slid out the photograph of the family with their old sedan parked by the ocean. She blew off a light film of dust and, sitting back on her heels, gazed at it again. "Why does this woman fascinate me so much?" she wondered aloud. She pushed herself up from the floor, hurried back down to the pantry and dug out the old bronze frame. Now just look at this, she laughed as she held the picture against the frame. It just fits!

She carried her prize out to the kitchen and laid it on the table, squatted down and opened the door to the cupboard under the sink, rattling around until she had found the Comet and Windex. She pried the frame apart, cleaned the bronze with Comet and a soft rag and polished the glass with Windex. At last, she slid in the photo and set the framed picture down in front of her.

Emily smiled at the photograph and the family smiled back. "This is where you belong, folks," she told them, and carried the frame to her office, putting it next to her wedding picture. She glanced at the officer then touched his face with one finger. For a minute her heart seemed to skip a beat and she shook her head and turned away. Now, what is wrong with me? She wondered, embarrassed, then forgot about it.

Now and again a group of visitors would brave the weather and arrive at the back door, knocking and peering through the screen, stamping the rain off their shoes and shaking their umbrellas when she let them in. Emily would smile, escort them through the kitchen and on to the rest of the house, and the visitors would look around in wonder.

"Wow," a little boy said, gazing at the boy's bedroom, "look at these awesome posters, and look, *look*, Daddy, a real antique Erector Set."

His father grimaced and winked at Emily. "Not so antique, Son. I had one of those when I was your age and it was my prized possession. Ha-ha-ho," he laughed awkwardly.

The women loved the kitchen and pantry, would fuss over the old Oatmeal cereal boxes and heavy green Depression glasses. "Oh, my, look at that Coke calendar," said a woman with dyed red hair in a short bob. "I remember one of those in the corner store when I was a little kid." Her friends gathered around and gushed over such memories, giggling and blushing like young girls.

Emily enjoyed listening to the tourists who were old enough to remember the things in History House.

However, the rain did keep people away and she had to keep herself busy going over her reports or wandering through the house. The clouds would lift now and again, and she'd dash out onto the fort grounds to walk around, get some exercise. Anything to break up the monotony, she'd complain as she slammed out the screen door.

One day Emily decided to walk past the other houses. Pulling a scarf over her hair, she set off down the street towards the parade ground, peering through the windows and into some of the houses lined up along the street. The grass was wet but had been mowed and some of the steps were repaired, but only History House and the Audubon Society house at Number 30 had been repaired.

On the way back, Emily picked her way across the grass to the garage attached to History House. The door was still intact, but it was swollen with age and humidity and jammed at an angle. There were two smudged glass windows and a rusty lock hanging off the side. On tiptoe, she reached up and tried to clean off some of the dirt from the windows. After rubbing furiously with a Kleenex, she peered through and wondered: what in the world kind of dirt is this? She rubbed some more, but the smears seemed to be etched into the glass. With some curiosity, Emily tried to pry the door open.

The more she tried the more it resisted. There's *got* to be something in here, she said, prying at one of the rusty hinges with her fingers, then prodded and pushed until, with a tired groan, the old door shuffled aside and Emily squeezed through the open space.

The garage was small and dark. The dirty windows allowed only dim light through; the cement floor was cracked and broken. Weeds grew between the cracks and there was a dank, damp smell. The walls were brick, and dust had settled in all the crevices. Emily squinted in the dim light and dusted off her khaki slacks. Yuck! What in the world possessed me to do *this*?

She squinted again and took a few steps further into the garage, peering through the dim light, then picked her way to the back of the space. A woman's bicycle was leaning against one of the dank walls. It was an old pre-World War II single-speed with balloon tires and a wire basket on the handlebars. The rubber tires were flat but not torn or ruined and seemed to be in good shape, and at one time it might have been a light blue, but now it was more rust than paint and somewhere along the line it had lost its stand.

Whoa, what have we *here*? Emily was excited. Neat old bike. Bet this old gal is still serviceable. With a good dose of that WD-40 and some elbow grease, I can get this in running order. She poked one of the tires. And if I can inflate these we'll be good to go. She pulled the bicycle away from the wall and wheeled it, creaking and bumping, through the door and up to the back steps of History House. Once I have this cute little antique cleaned and in working order, I'll be able to explore Fort Hancock from one end to the other.

The thought gave Emily's heart a lift, a sudden sense of adventure. "This old blue bike is my ticket to freedom," she said out loud and never gave a thought to who might have owned the bicycle and why it had been left to rust in the old garage.

CHAPTER TWENTY-ONE

THE BLUE BICYCLE

1944

STEWART AND MABEL Schmidt had met in Broken Bow Grade School, a one-story brick building that stood at the edge of town. Stewart was in fifth grade and Mabel one grade behind. Both of them lived on farms outside of town and, along with the other Nebraska farm offspring, took the faded yellow school bus that rumbled up the dusty road, picked them up as they waited on Rural Route 1 and brought them, books, sack lunches and all, into town, depositing them in the dusty yard outside Broken Bow Grade School.

Even in fifth grade, Stewart had been a handsome boy, tall and blond with mischievous blue eyes that gleamed with fun. Mabel was small and blond with long, thick braids and suntanned legs that could outrace anyone in Broken Bow Grade School, including Stewart. By the time they were in high school, Stewart and Mabel had become an item, "going steady," Mabel told her girlfriends in confidence. She wore Stewart's class ring on a gold chain around her neck and refused to take it off, even when she donned her cheerleading outfit to cheer for Broken Bow's high school football team.

When he graduated from high school in the class of 1939, Stewart told Mabel that what he really wanted to be was a doctor, but his family didn't have the money to send him to the university, "and of course there is the war"; so he charmed his way into working for Mr. Sullivan in the pharmacy of the new Sullivan Drugs on Main Street in Broken Bow. "If I can't be a doctor, he told Mabel, "I can be a pharmacist and help people that way."

Stewart and Mabel were married in the Broken Bow Methodist Church on June 14, 1941. "I always wanted to be a June bride," Mabel told her girlfriends while waiting for Mrs. Drum, her hat bobbing up and down in the choir loft, to start the wedding march on the church's pump organ.

Then, at 7:55 a.m. on December 7, the Japanese dropped more than two hundred tons of bombs on Pearl Harbor, and at 12:30 p.m. the next day the President of the United States declared war on Japan. Soon after, Stewart was drafted and left Broken Bow for basic training. He was assigned to the Medical Corps and went to school to learn how to bandage a sucking chest wound and stabilize shattered bones with an M1 carbine and yards of gauze bandage.

In 1943, Stewart was ordered to Fort Hancock in far-off New Jersey and, using their savings, brought Mabel to live in a small first-floor apartment, one room and a tiny kitchen, in a widow's home on the mainland near the Highlands Bridge. Along with her fabric, sewing basket and clothes, Mabel insisted on bringing her new blue bicycle, a gift from her husband.

"You will be living at Fort Hancock in the barracks," she told him bravely, "I can ride around the town to keep busy." So the bicycle rode in the baggage car on the same train with Mabel, all the way from Nebraska to the coast of New Jersey.

A few weeks after the incident with Della and the submarine, James brought Betty a bicycle. Down at the bottom of the want-ads page in the Army Times, he had spotted a little entry: *Almost new. Blue woman's bicycle. Perfect condition. Owner is moving home while her husband is overseas. Good price. Ask for PFC Schmidt at SH5-9441 Extension 4502.*

Now, there's a good idea, James thought to himself, and carefully circled the advertisement with his fountain pen. That morning, he called the phone number and talked to the young soldier. "I'm interested in the bicycle," he said, and offered a reasonable amount.

The young man thought about it for a bit and then agreed. "Yeah, that's okay. My unit's leaving in two weeks for the South Pacific and my wife's moving back to Nebraska to stay with her parents." He paused for a minute. "They have a big farm and plenty of room. Mabel's bicycle is in good shape and she loves it, but she can't very well take it on the bus with her and we sure can't afford the train now." He gave a short laugh. "We're selling everything we bought here. Do you need a set of dishes? An almost-new bedspread?"

James felt sorry for the young soldier. So many of these youngsters were being sent overseas; so many were never going to come home. "We don't need a bedspread or any dishes," he said softly, "but the bicycle is for my wife. She's not very happy since we came here and she's taken to wandering off the base and down to the shore. I'm hoping the bicycle will give her a boost, make her little trips more fun. You can tell your wife her bicycle will be in good and loving hands." He paused for a minute and then added, "I promise!"

That afternoon, he drove onto the mainland and met PFC Schmidt at the little house where the wife lived. James pulled his wallet out of his back pocket and took out some money.

"This is a dang hard time," the young solider confided to James. He tipped his cap back and scratched his head. He was a tall, sturdy man. His blond hair, with its army regulation haircut, and faded blue eyes spoke of the plains and wheat fields of the Midwest. "My wife and me, we was married just before Pearl Harbor," he said softly. "I never imagined we'd be in such a situation." He shuffled his foot in the dust. "Back in Nebraska," he continued, "I was learning to be a pharmacist, and now I'm going to God-knows-where as a medic. Medicine, anyway, I guess."

He wheeled the bicycle out to the car and stood back as James took a heavy rope out of the trunk. As he tied the bicycle onto the bumper of his sedan, James saw the soldier's wife, standing at the window, her face sad in the afternoon sun. He drove away with his heart heavy for the young couple.

Betty was thrilled with the bicycle. When he pulled into the driveway, she had just come in from picking tomatoes from her Victory Garden and was washing them in the kitchen sink. "James," she laughed excitedly when she saw it, "This is just *swell*. I can ride around the fort, and look, Dear, it has a basket! I can even pack a lunch and go down to the shore to swim." She threw her arms around him and hugged him hard. "I didn't *dream* that you would do this. What a wonderful surprise!" James hugged her back and Betty felt her anxiety fall away.

Every day Betty polished the bicycle's blue paint and shiny chrome bars and wiped the rubber tires with one of her husband's old army shirts. It gave her more freedom to roam the dirt roads outside the main gates and to find new shorelines to explore. At night she stored it in the garage by the house and carefully locked the garage door. "You can never be too careful," she told James.

In the morning, as soon as her husband's staff car drove away, she'd wheel her bicycle out and park it next to the back steps. After the children were safely at the Army Children's Center, she'd put on a pair of blue shorts and a white navy-style shirt and push her bicycle out to the road by the open field.

She'd ride across the fort and pass the enlisted men's barracks: rows of wooden buildings, long and low, lined with shuttered windows and painted a bright, light yellow, standing and facing the ocean side of the fort. White pines, planted during WWI, grew among the buildings.

The road continued around the brick Officers' Club, with its big windows, wide veranda and black iron fire escape. Just past the Officers' Club were the Service Center and Enlisted Men's Club for the enlisted men and their wives or girlfriends; here the road connected to the central street that led to the Main Gate. As Betty pedaled along, the other wives would smile at her, and as she passed the guards at the gates, they'd whistle and wave.

Then she would be outside and on the dirt roads that led down to the shore on one side and the bay on the other.

Some days she'd ride down to the bay and would sit for hours looking across the water to the mainland, thinking about how isolated they all were here at Fort Hancock.

Other times she turned left and followed the winding, overgrown paths to the ocean, leaving her bike against one of the stunted trees that grew on the sandy hillocks. Piling her shoes and socks by her bicycle, Betty would walk across the hot sand and wade along the shoreline. From the beach, she could look out over the ocean with its waves breaking just offshore, and the clouds as they rolled up from the horizon. Standing there with the sky and the sea, Betty would feel as if there were no war, no air raids, no rations. "I wonder if James has any idea how much his gift has changed my life," she wondered aloud as she swished her feet back and forth in the surf. Della and her rumors began to recede into the distance.

CHAPTER TWENTY-TWO

THE OLD MORTAR BATTERY

JUNE 2009

B Y THE END of the week, the bicycle was scrubbed and polished, the chain and wheels oiled, the basket cleared of dried leaves, gum wrappers and an old telephone bill. The day was overcast, but the rain seemed to be holding off, so during her lunch hour Emily walked the bicycle to the side of the road by the field and, with a cheering group of grounds workers watching, pushed off with a wobbling start. It took her a few minutes to get it moving, swaying dangerously from one side to another. "My God," she said under her breath, "how in the world did anyone haul themselves around on these things?"

Still wobbling, she headed up the main road that crossed the fort and was soon cruising by the old yellow barracks. By the time she had reached the dilapidated Officer's Club, she felt comfortable enough to pull up and hop off. Leaning the bicycle against the side of the building, she walked around to the huge double doors at the front.

The Officer's Club was big: a Victorian-style brick house with a wide veranda that ran around the front and down one side of the building. An old, rusted fire escape zigzagged up the wall and hung drunkenly off the bricks just under a top window.

Emily climbed the steps and rubbed dust off one of the front windows with a tissue. "Wow, awesome," she whispered as she looked into what was obviously a nightclub. The old wooden bar was still standing, its heavy mahogany presence taking up the length of the room. A huge, rust-stained mirror filled the wall behind the bar and a number of empty shelves were covered with dust. Chairs were piled on small, round tables next to a wooden dance floor and a padded swinging door hung half open.

I bet there were a whole bunch of parties in *that* room, she thought, and rubbed another space in the window, craning her neck for a better look. The walls were covered with tattered red wallpaper; faded red drapes hung from brass curtain rods above the smudged, dusty windows. Brushing her hands off, Emily walked back across the veranda and down the front steps. Somewhere nearby she heard faint, tinny music as if one of the grounds' crew was playing an old transistor radio... but the fort was empty and still.

She spent her lunch hour exploring one building after another until she realized with a start that she had spent more than two hours wandering the fort. "Rats," she grumbled and, clambering onto the heavy bicycle, turned around and pedaled her way back to the museum as fast as the ancient bike would go. As the old buildings were left behind, she found herself singing: *I don't know why I love you but I do, I don't know why I cry so but I do, I only know I'm lonely and that I want you only...* That's odd, she whispered, I wonder where *that* came from?

Emily had become more comfortable in her job. As she came through the door each morning, she'd drop her pocketbook on her desk, plug in the coffeepot and spend the best part of the morning dusting the rooms and putting out brochures. By then, her coffee would be brewed, and she would settle into her office with a fresh cup, checking over the paperwork needing her attention. Now and then, John Rogers would call and they'd chat for a few minutes, catching up on National Park news and what updates he felt she needed "way out on the peninsula," as he called Fort Hancock.

More than once he asked if she had heard any more sounds. "So, any more footsteps from upstairs?" he'd asked, or "Are you hearing any…uh…voices or anything?" She'd hear his chuckle over the phone.

Emily decided to keep the sounds and voices to herself, and would laugh, "Nope, no more sounds, no voices. I guess the ghost isn't restless anymore."

But, truth be told, she had, indeed, started hearing voices. Sometimes it would be a soft sigh; other times she could almost hear words in the sound of the rain as it drifted across the bay. By now, she had stopped searching the house, would just sit at her desk and continue filling out her paperwork. It didn't bother her anymore.

Whenever the weather cleared, she'd roll the blue bicycle out of the garage and head out across Fort Hancock on her lunch hour, exploring this strange corner of Sandy Hook.

One gray day she found the ancient cannon she'd seen in the photograph, green with age but still pointing majestically out to sea. She thought about the young soldiers and wondered if any of them were still alive. They were just kids, she thought as she inspected the huge weapon, young and so full of life, but no… that was, my God, almost a hundred years ago. She ran her hand over the rusted cannon and shook her head in wonder. She visited Sandy Hook Lighthouse with its bright white paint and attached red-roofed barracks. John had told her it had been restored in 2000 and now there was talk it would be used as a backdrop for *Guiding Light*, a soap opera she remembered from her teens. Beautiful, she thought as she gazed up at the tall octagonal tower, its metal railing and peaked-hatted lamp at the top, this lighthouse has seen so much history and so much beauty and tragedy out on the ocean.

Another afternoon she came upon a strange and mysterious place. Behind a copse of trees and gorse bushes she spotted an old structure: high stone walls covered with moss and twigs, rusted iron railings and ancient steps that led down from a stone bridge, a windowless hut perched on top. Eerie silence seemed to hang over everything.

Emily leaned the bike against the iron fence and picked her way down the worn stone steps into the structure. What in the world is this place? she wondered as she wandered under the bridge. Corroded railroad tracks led along a cobblestone path and disappeared into a tunnel in the embankment. Emily stood looking into the dark opening with interest, then shivered. It seemed to her the darkness was too deep, too intense, almost alive. She shook her head and tried to clear her mind. What is wrong with me? she wondered. Sometimes I feel like I'm beginning to lose it.

The rain started up again and sent her pedaling back to History House. One day, she thought, one of these days, I'll come back and explore that tunnel. Then added, if I dare.

"Oh, that," John Rogers said later the same afternoon. "I think it's another old mortar battery. Wild place, lots of underbrush." He warmed to the subject. "I believe they may have plans to restore more of those in the future, too. Just be careful you don't fall down the stairs. Yes, be careful!"

After she hung up, Emily sat looking out over the grounds, rolling a pencil around in her fingers and listening to quiet steps tiptoeing across the hall overhead. She was beginning to realize there was more to this old army fort than she'd been told. Right then and there, she decided she was the one to learn its secrets.

What she didn't realize was how much she really *would* learn about Fort Hancock and where it would take her.

CHAPTER TWENTY-THREE

BETTY AND ANNA

1943-1945

A T Fort Hancock the officers' wives had housekeepers, nice women who came from the mainland and cleaned and babysat the children when asked. Betty's housekeeper, Anna, was Polish. She had fled Poland in the fall of 1939, just as the Nazis invaded.

Her family had stayed behind, and one day Anna confided, in her broken English, "I don't know what happen to my family. I don't even know if they still be alive."

Betty was shocked. She had never really thought about Anna's life or the path she had traveled to come to America. The two women were sitting in the kitchen, polishing the silverware. Betty put down the fork she was working on and looked at Anna with a sense of alarm. "What? Anna, is your family still in Poland?" She had always assumed the young woman lived with her parents on the mainland.

Anna's eyes filled with tears and she took a tissue out of her apron pocket and dried them. "We were told to leave, one night very late. The neighbors, they come and knock on door, say 'run, run, peoples' and my father, he give me a bundle with clothes, moneys and told me, 'Go, Anna, go and we come next.' " She stopped for a minute and swallowed hard, looking out the window. "They never come," she said softly. "I go on train and big boat to America, but they never come. I don't know if they still in Poland or even live." Betty felt terrible. She was always kind to Anna, bringing her a candy bar from the PX or giving her a dress or skirt from her own closet, but now she felt sick, empty. She didn't tell the other wives how she felt because they would certainly not approve.

"Housekeepers are for housekeeping," they said and usually ignored their housekeepers altogether.

But not Betty. She and Anna always sat down for lunch together on the days when Anna was cleaning the house. Betty made sandwiches from Spam, canned meat that the frugal Americans bought during the war years. She toasted white bread in the little silver toaster and spread each slice with oleomargarine. She fried the Spam and brewed tea in a china pot. Sometimes she would pick fresh tomatoes from her Victory Garden. She and Anna would sit by the kitchen window that looked out over the grounds and eat the sandwiches and tomatoes and drink the tea. It was during these quiet times that Betty learned about Europe's slow march into war.

"At first the young mens in the town, they start to march with flags and shouting strong things," Anna said, putting her sandwich down and picking up her tea. "Then, one day, they start to shouting terrible things about the Jewish peoples. My family doctor is Jewish and is fine man with wife and family." Anna stopped, sniffed and looked out the window again.

Betty had heard of the terrible things Adolf Hitler had done, but she'd never heard anything from the people who had actually lived with this evil. Never heard what it was like to live in one of the European countries in the run-up to war.

Anna looked back at Betty and continued in a soft voice, "My father and mother, they bring food and wine to our doctor at his home because doctor, he is scared to go to store, and my father, he then speak out loud at town hall about the bad way our Jewish neighbors and friends, they are being treated. Tells people it very, very bad and evil. Jewish people, they are Polish people like us."

Betty's eyes widened. "They were afraid to go *outside* to the *store,*" she said, shaking her head in disbelief.

Anna nodded. "They afraid to go out, so nobody to hurt them. Then in fall time, with leaves in color, friends come to our house and say, 'Hitler comes now so run, run, run.' So, I run, but I not see my family again."

Betty patted Anna's hand. "Your family will come here soon, right here to America," she told her firmly, "They will come and then you will all be a family again, safe here in America." Betty didn't know if this would be true, but she could only hope and pray; so hope and pray she did as the days and weeks passed.

One morning Betty was mixing yellow food coloring into a new package of oleomargarine and waiting for Anna to finish the upstairs bedrooms. "Oleo duty," as she called it, was not an unusual task during the war and, although she hated it, she felt it had to be done. "This is such a waste of time," she grumbled, "but who wants that awful white oleomargarine on their toast? Ugh!"

One of the women in the wives club, whose family owned a dairy farm in Wisconsin, had told them about the "Butter Wars". "Years and years ago the dairy farmers forced congress to pass laws to put margarine out of business," she told them. "We don't need fake yellow spread to ruin us, you know. Congress passed taxes and tariffs and even some "No Yellow Color Law" so those margarine people couldn't add color." She sniffed, "so the margarine factories put these little food coloring packets inside the margarine packages and we have to mix it ourselves. Now look what's happening, butter is rationed and too expensive and we all have to use margarine."

Betty thought it was pretty silly and had said as much that evening when James came home. "I'm sick of wars," she'd complained, "World War One and World War Two and now a Butter War on oleomargarine. I think it's silly. When will it stop?

Why don't they just make it yellow in the factories, at least for the war effort."

And as the color swirled through the margarine she had to agree with herself, again.

When Anna was finished upstairs, she joined Betty in the kitchen. She washed her hands in the sink and dried them on a hand towel and was smiling when she sat down.

"I receive letter from my brother," she said. "He is in Canada with father and mother. Maybe they comes soon to America. Then we can be family again." She wiped her eyes with the edge of the towel. Betty leaned across the table, touching Anna's hand gently. "I thought you looked cheerful today," she said happily. "I heard you singing upstairs. Families need to stay together." And she held that thought in her heart as the war dragged on.

Anna babysat on Friday nights and James would take Betty out for the evening, sometimes to the Officers' Club for drinks and dinner. The Officers' Club was in a huge, Victorian building that sat on a smooth, green patch of lawn. When they entered through the big double doors, a smartly dressed butler would take their wraps and hang them in a large closet. There were flowers in the foyer; a Persian rug covered the tiled floor. The nightclub was a wonderful, spacious room with a carved wooden bar and gilded mirror that took up the whole wall. Glistening bottles sat on long shelves, lit from below. The walls were papered in lush, red wallpaper, and heavy dark red drapes hung on all the windows. Chairs and tables were grouped around a small dance floor, and at the end of the room a padded swinging door led to the kitchen.

James and Betty would join other couples and as the men talked about the war, the women gossiped about their children, food shortages and, of course, housekeepers and when the little band played slow songs, they'd slip out onto the dance floor, holding each other close as they swayed with the music, Betty softly singing along: *I don't know why I love you but I do, I don't know why I cry so but I do, I only know I'm lonely and that I want you only…* These were the good times and she knew she would always remember them.

Betty and the other wives tried to avoid the war talk, wanting to keep it at bay and out of their own lives, but too often someone would share a rumor and that would scare all of them. Betty closed her ears to such things and the next day she would ride her blue bike out to the dirt roads and along the shore, trying to forget the rumor she had heard the night before.

Other times, James and Betty went to the small movie theater on Fort Hancock to enjoy the latest films: comedies that made them laugh and musicals, filled with singing and dancing, cheering up the war-weary Americans. Before the movie feature, the "Movietone Newsreel" of the week would run: loud, patriotic music and reel upon reel of tanks and airplanes, bombs falling through the clouds, turning into puffs of smoke on the ground below and the ack-ack sound of the returning fire. Betty didn't like the newsreels, she couldn't help but think about the children down there or the boys, so vulnerable in their planes high above, but she would sing "America the Beautiful" and shout Rah! Rah! Rah with the rest of the audience when an American bomb destroyed the enemy.

As much as she disliked these short news films, from them she learned what was happening in Europe, the South Pacific and North Africa: that France had surrendered to Nazi Germany in June of 1940 and Nazi Germany had marched into Paris, occupying much of France's territory; that fighting in North Africa had started with the declaration of war by Italy and that Japan had invaded French Indochina. Awful things that frightened her.

A few weeks after the newsreel on the German invasion of France, an update was introduced by a French official who explained: "What is left of free France has established a new

French Fascist-leaning government based in Vichy. Thank you very much." He tweaked his neat mustache. "This is Vichy France and will be officially known as The French State. We are proud to support Hitler, Mussolini and the three Axis powers. The French North be damned!" he ended pompously and the news moved on. Betty thought he was very snobbish and didn't like him at all; added to that, he was aiding the enemy.

"James, why would he *do* such a thing," she whispered, outraged. "He's supposed to be *our* friend, not Hitler's."

James took her hand and gently rubbed her fingers. "War does strange things to people. I don't know. I can't answer your question. We just have to do our best, Baby. He leaned down and kissed her palm."

The newsreels kept coming and in July of 1943 she learned that Mussolini, the Italian dictator, had been thrown out of power and into prison; then the newsreels began to announce the American victories over the Japanese in the Pacific and this lifted Betty's heart.

Finally, after four years of European occupation and strife, Allied forces, including Free-French forces from the north, liberated all of France from the Germans and the streets were filled with cheering crowds, exhausted by the German occupation and separation of their country. Men, women and children shouting, "We are free again. France is ours again," tossed flowers to the Allied soldiers in the trucks and jeeps as they sped through the towns. In the spring of 1945, the newsreels were filled with the Allies marching into city after European city as the German troops limped out, long lines of ragged and exhausted soldiers following the retreating trucks and tanks.

When that news of American victories flashed across the screen, Betty applauded with the rest of the audience, and she meant it! For every allied victory, the possibility that her husband would not have to go overseas became stronger.

The wives in the Officer's Club and at afternoon teas started to whisper rumors of a deadly new weapon, one that would surely bring an end to this endless war.

"It's something new, something really big and powerful."

"But what, a bomb?"

"I don't know and my husband doesn't tell me. All I know is it will amaze the world and maybe kill a lot of people."

"Well, as long as it ends this terrible war, I don't care what it does. I'm sorry, but I really don't care!"

Betty was uneasy but relieved. "I don't want anymore killing and dying. I just want to go home," she whispered back.

As the April days turned balmier, Betty and the people she saw every day felt more and more hopeful and she could hear the children laughing more often as they played upstairs, hear little James telling Bobbie about the pretty purple mountains back home.

CHAPTER TWENTY-FOUR

THE KIDS UPSTAIRS

JULY 2009

JULY ARRIVED AND the rain left without a backward glance. Mornings dawned bright and the days became hot and dry. The air was still, with no breeze until late in the day. Everything smelled of dust. In the evening, the sky would turn into a firestorm of color as the sun sank in the west, and the grass would rustle with the breeze off the water.

Emily had decided to plant some tomatoes outside her house in Atlantic Highlands. She'd bought the little seedlings in June and kept them in the kitchen window. Now, with the warm weather and sunshine, she was able to carry them outside and plant them by the house, scooping the damp earth out with a large spoon and setting in each plant. When the last one was in the ground, she stood up, brushing a lock of hair out of her eyes. Nice! My New Jersey tomatoes. Yummy! That Saturday she told Derek about her little garden. "Some real *hardy* New Jersey tomatoes, she said, "like a Victory Garden."

"A Victory Garden?" Derek's finger touched the screen and Emily responded with her own forefinger, almost like holding hands, she thought. "It sounds like you're really getting into this World War Two stuff. I look forward to some of these Jersey tomatoes when I get home." He moved his finger over the screen and added, "that's not all I'm looking forward to when I get home," and they smiled at each other across so many miles of ocean and desert.

Emily was finally able to dress in light summer clothes: cool cotton pants and cotton shirts with her blond curls tucked under a headband. With a sense of relief, she packed her sweaters and wool slacks in the cedar chest and washed and ironed her summer clothing. When she stopped at the Coffee Bean she'd saunter into the coffee shop instead of dodging raindrops, and ask for iced coffee.

"Hi, Pretty Lady." The counterman would hand her coffee, smiling and waiting for her flirtatious response.

Emily would toss her curls and bat her eyelashes. "Hi, Kiddo, you make my day," she'd tell him, and he actually did!

History House welcomed the warm weather. Emily spent the first hour every morning opening the windows and dusting off the windowsills. "Good old house," she'd say loudly, in case "someone" was listening, "You're a wonderful summer place." She tied back the curtains and worked at the stubborn old windows until they were open to the summer heat. The house was not air-conditioned, but there were fans in each room, and with the high ceilings and wide veranda, it stayed surprisingly comfortable. She'd move through the rooms turning on the fans: first downstairs and then in the upstairs bedrooms. The only room she stayed away from was the officer's study. There were too many valuable and fragile antiques to take a chance and, she had to admit, she was still haunted by the strange longing and apprehension she had experienced the first day. This is one place I want to stay away from, she admitted, and she'd walk around the open door and continue tidying the rest of the big house.

One morning she tried to scrub the chalk notation off the blackboard outside the kitchen. It wouldn't budge. Whoa! What in the world kind of chalk did this person use? she thought, puzzled, and hunted under the sink until she found the can of Comet. But even the Comet didn't scrub the notation off. Crap, she said and put the can away.

As the weather warmed up, so did the sounds in the officer's house. Sometimes it sounded like a crowd gathering in the hall upstairs. Occasionally footsteps would tap across the floor in the hall overhead, then start down the stairs. In the evening, she'd hear a whispered word or a soft laugh. This house is more alive than my own, she mused, but rarely gave it a thought and never bothered to tell John Rogers when he stopped by. "How's it going, young lady?" he'd ask with raised eyebrows, waiting for her to fill him in on the mysterious sounds. Much to his relief, Emily had nothing to say and they would go on to other business.

When visitors arrived, the voices would be still and as the guests followed her through the rooms she'd smile, knowing that as soon as she was alone the strange goings-on would start up again, but one afternoon that changed.

The last tour group of the day gathered their belongings before heading out to their cars, chattering among themselves. Emily was tired but pleased with the afternoon and was counting noses when a young women, her tousled hair in a red headscarf, broke away from the group. "Allan! Where are you? Where's my son? He was right behind me on the stairs." She began to look frightened and the group milled around nervously. Emily followed her as she hurried into the hall. "He was right behind me. I knew I shouldn't come alone. His father would never allow this, never!" She wrung her hands.

A small boy was sitting on the stairs, his crew cut standing up in blond spikes, busy with a Game Boy and paying no attention. Ah! Emily thought, obviously Allan. His mother sent him a furious look, hissed, "Allan, darn it, where in the world were you?" She snatched the Game Boy and pushed him ahead of her into the kitchen. "We're getting ready to leave and you disappear. You're not being fair at all and Mommy is very disappointed with you. Yes, very disappointed. Wait till I tell your father!" Embarrassed, she took a tissue and snuffled into it and Emily thought: uh oh!

Allan looked back at his mother, incensed. "Hey, I was upstairs with those kids. We were in the boy's room."

Emily frowned and looked at the faces gathered around her: three elderly couples, a foreign student from Rutgers and Allan's mother. Kids, what kids? Who else had children with them? She couldn't remember any other children and Allan was now scowling sullenly by the door. "What kids, Allan?" She smiled encouragement. "Who were they with? Is there anyone else up there?"

He shrugged, frowned, "you know, those kids that live upstairs." He looked down at his empty hands and then up at her. "And guess what? Those dumb kids don't even know what a Game Boy is. Funny kids, you know? They're boring."

His mother turned red and marched him out the door, the tour group close on her heals. "He does this all the time. He makes thing up, tells stories. He sees things. Wait till I tell his father!"

Emily didn't say anything more, but closed the door after the group, deep in thought.

Later, as she was locking up for the night, she heard a man's voice: One word, then two, then silence. Emily frowned and walked back to the study, expecting to see John Rogers standing by her desk, but everything was quiet. The office was empty. This was the first time she'd heard a man's voice and Emily thought: first *those kids upstairs* and now a man's voice. "Huh, odd," She said aloud to the empty office.

On the way down Hartshorne Drive, she turned to a country and western station, Ray Price singing of loss and heartbreak, and fleetingly wondered when she had started to hunger for these old, soulful country ballads. She arrived at home that evening with an odd feeling of anxiety.

CHAPTER TWENTY-FIVE

TRAILER HOMES

JULY 2009

EMILY DROVE OVER the bridge and turned north, the windows open and the radio turned to a music station. It was another breathless Tuesday morning in early July, and as she approached the base she was surprised to see a number of trailer homes pulled up among the trees. Besides bird-watchers and occasional hikers, this section of Sandy Hook had been empty since she'd been coming to Fort Hancock. The appearance of the trailers puzzled her. Could they have arrived during the weekend? She slowed down and peered out of the window. "Hello," she called, "anybody home?"

The trailer homes seemed unoccupied in their stillness, but here and there wash was hanging on lines and pots of flowers lined the sides of the foundations. Toys were scattered on the grass and sand; in the distance Emily could hear children's voices over the sound of the waves. Everyone's down on the beach, she thought as she took her foot off the brake. Whoever has arrived over the weekend will surely announce themselves soon enough.

She turned away and the trailer homes were left behind. The thought of the families living next to Fort Hancock warmed her heart. How odd, she thought. Why would these trailer homes lift my spirits? I'm actually becoming…what…lonely? She hummed along with the radio. I like the idea of some real people living out in those trailers.

She spent the rest of the day with tourists, showing them around; telling them stories of Fort Hancock and History House. By now she felt she was welcoming guests into her own home. She'd begun to change her looks as well. Instead of the light pink lip blush, she had stopped by the CVS in town and found one called Cherry Red. Her blond curls were beginning to grow out and she pulled them back with a wide headband. When she looked at herself in the mirror she decided she approved. The tourists seemed to enjoy her new look, too. "Awesome, like you belong to this old house," said a gawky teenaged girl.

When the last of the visitors had left, Emily gathered up the brochures, closed the windows and pulled the drapes. I wonder if the families are back in their trailer homes, she thought as she picked up her pocketbook and headed for the door. They must be back from the beach by now. She drove toward the gate filled with anticipation. If the occupants are back from the beach, I'll stop and introduce myself, let them know I'm working right up the road at Fort Hancock, maybe invite myself for coffee. She smiled at the thought.

Emily would never meet the people in the trailer homes; when she pulled up next to the copse of trees, they were gone. The sand was smooth and untouched and there was no trace of the trailer homes or their occupants among the trees and no sign they had ever been there.

CHAPTER TWENTY-SIX

THE WAR BRIDES

1944

BETTY SLIPPED ON her bathing suit, retrieved her blue bicycle from the garage and headed for the front gate. It was another breathless morning in early July and the air was heavy with the heat. She was looking forward to a dip in the ocean and pedaled hard past the MPs at the gate and out onto the post road. As she came around the bend, she was startled to see a number of trailer homes standing among the trees. They seemed unoccupied in their stillness; here and there wash was hanging on lines, and pots of flowers lined the sides of the homes. Toys were scattered on the grass and sand. In the distance, she heard children's voices over the sound of the waves on the shore.

She passed the trailers and continued down the path to the beach. As she pulled up onto a bank above the shore, she saw a number of young women sitting on a blanket, chatting and laughing among themselves. Nearby, blond and tanned children were digging in the sand and dashing into the waves. As she came closer, Betty heard their strange accent and it occurred to her that these were the young Australian war brides the officers' wives had been talking about, living here outside Fort Hancock and far from home.

United States troops had started pouring into Australia on Christmas Eve, 1941. The American sailors and soldiers made friends wherever they went, and the Australian people didn't hesitate to offer hospitality and friendship to their American cousins; however, the American troops were better paid and, with their access to all the wonderful items in their PX, they were able to live more lavishly and comfortably than the local Australians. This in turn led to many Australian women preferring the Americans, and a number of the U.S. servicemen fell in love with the pretty young Australians, married them and sent them home to the United States. Of course, this didn't sit well with their Australian hosts. But, here they were!

Betty slowed down to look at the strangers. Oh, boy, she thought, and we thought we felt isolated and homesick. Stopping next to a gorse bush, she kicked the bicycle stand down, pulled off her shorts and top and piled them next to her bicycle. She smoothed her bathing suit over her hips and started down the sand toward the ocean, glancing at the group and sending a small, welcoming smile their way.

The young women smiled back as she walked past, and one of them patted the blanket next to her. "Please, sit, sit," she said. "We like America, we like Americans."

Betty squatted down next to her. "I'm going to swim. Do you go into the water?" Australia was so foreign and far away, she had no idea what it was like or, to be honest, where it actually was. She knew all about France and England, even Germany and Japan, but not the part of the world that these young mothers were from. She paused, wanting to engage these strangers, "Where are you girls from?"

The women laughed and glanced at each other. "We're from Australia, way on the other side of the world, and yes, we sure do swim." A pretty blond woman looked up from the blanket. In her strange, clipped accent she added, "We swim and ride horses, too, along the sand, sometimes into the water."

A stocky young woman with short strawberry-blond curls sat up and leaned on one elbow. "Where we come from there's the biggest ocean in the world at our front door. Unless we're from in-country, of course. We all learn to swim by the time we're knee high to a grass-oppa." The others laughed at this and again offered Betty a space on their blanket.

Betty smiled and shook her head. "I don't know anything about Australia. I've never been to any other countries. Are you happy here in America?"

The pretty blond smiled a sad smile. "Yes, we all like America, but we are homesick. We miss our mums and dads. We miss our families and friends back home." She rubbed her eye with a finger.

"But we all have each other," one of the other women added. "We're all friends here so we're never lonely." She leaned over and put her arm around her friend and then patted the blanket. "Here, Mrs. American, we have room on our blanket for one more. Why don't you join us?"

Betty smiled, shook her head again, and headed across the sand. As she paddled around in the ocean and splashed into the surf, she waved at the young wives and they laughed and waved back.

"Swim, swim," they called. "Swim, Mrs. American," but none of them joined her in the water and as much as she longed to share their blankets and learn more about their lives, she kept her distance, filled with an odd shyness. They're enlisted men's wives, she told herself, it isn't right for me to intrude.

As the sun began to sink over the trees, Betty ducked behind the gorse bush and changed out of her wet swimsuit. On her way home, she looked back and waved as she wheeled her bicycle up the dirt road. "Good bye, girls," she called. "Good bye, Mrs. American," they called back. "Come back soon and join us by the big ocean. We like Americans."

Betty decided not to tell James about the Australian war brides on the beach. Even though he was a kind and gentle man, she felt her husband would never approve of her having spent time on the beach with a group of enlisted men's foreign wives... wives that lived in a trailer camp.

CHAPTER TWENTY-SEVEN

ROBIN DRURY

JULY 2009

O N WARM SUMMER afternoons, Emily would wander out onto the broad veranda and stand gazing out over the bay. She enjoyed the changing face of the water, the sunset and the shadows chasing themselves across the seawall, the lights starting to blink on over on the mainland.

One hot and humid afternoon she was suddenly gripped by a restless melancholy. The sun had just disappeared into a western cloudbank, and as the last rays slipped out of sight, she saw the stranger standing at the edge of the bay, twisting a ring on her left hand. She was dressed in a red-and-white sundress and her dark hair was turned under in a neat pageboy. Emily was baffled by how familiar this stranger seemed.

Do I know this woman? Is she in my yoga class? She tucked a lock of her hair behind her ear. I bet I've seen her on the mainland, shopping, or in town. She shook her head, mystified. Once again, she longed to join her, but turned and slipped back into the living room. This stranger was so alone, so unapproachable. Emily just couldn't get up the courage to cross the lawn and introduce herself. Someday, she promised herself, someday I'll walk over and say hello.

She moved from one room to another closing the windows and drawing the drapes. The sun rays were now moving over the bay, filling the big room with shadows. And then, she heard the soft laughter again. Emily stopped and held her breath, thought: Where? The kitchen? This time she felt a presence nearby. Okay, what in the world's going on here? She hurried through the pantry, but nothing was moving except the curtains, swaying in the open kitchen windows. She walked back through the pantry, into the dining room, and through the living room, shouting, "Hello, hello," even peering through the windows onto the veranda.

As suddenly as it appeared, the presence was gone and the house was empty again; nothing stirred outside except the dry grass, rustling in the breeze. Emily glanced back at the seawall, but it was empty, too. Puzzled and slightly anxious, she went back to close the kitchen windows and stopped as she came through the door. On the kitchen table was a handful of wildflowers, their leaves wilting in the heat. Now where did these come from, she grumbled as she filled a glass vase and stuffed the flowers in the water. She gathered her bag and keys from her office, but as she turned the key in the Honda's ignition, she realized two things: She was less afraid of a ghost than she was of a living, breathing human being; and second, she wouldn't be joking about the officer's house, again...ever!

Robin Drury leaned across the table and paused for dramatic affect: "And then I left the coffee shop without even asking his name!" Emily Craig and Rebecca Wade were sitting across from her, fascinated by another of Robin's adventures.

Emily and Rebecca had spent Saturday afternoon at the Garden State Mall off the Garden State Parkway, had stopped for coffee and a light supper at Starbucks by the front entrance. Robin found them there and immediately joined them at the small table. "Wait, wait," she shouted as she arrived, dropping her bundles by the empty chair and dashing off to get a brewed "just old-fashioned ol' coffee, dark, no sugar."

Robin was one of Rebecca's acquaintances from her local Presbyterian Church, and was unlike any church member Emily had ever met. She was a tall, dark-haired beauty, with an abundance of curves that she used to her advantage. The loyalty she felt to First Presbyterian far outweighed that which she had felt for her ex-husband, a kindly, mousy bank manager in the next town. Robin drove the highways and byways of New Jersey in her red Miata convertible, her eye out for any young, attractive "gentleman" she could befriend. Despite her peccadilloes, Robin was a good-hearted woman. Her other passion was for the various charities she supported: "Help for Haitian Flood Victims," "The Wild Horse Sanctuary in Idaho" and "Homes for Felines." These she threw herself into with as much zeal as she did her other ventures.

Rebecca and Emily sat stunned at Robin's latest tale. Robin, noting their reaction, quickly changed the subject, regaling them instead with an enthusiastic overview of her latest fundraiser: a Saturday-evening gala with "all the fixings'" being held in an upscale restaurant nearby. Robin's latest event, to "Save the Timber Wolves in Montana," featured a well-known activist who was raising funds to enable the move of independent wolf cubs into safer surroundings away from the Montana ranchers.

Emily nibbled on a croissant. Rebecca smiled brightly as Robin continued her description of white tablecloths, good china, silverware and a "tasty menu." "Tasteful but simple," she told them, as she fanned her face with her hand. "Why am I so hot? Oh, no, not *that*…! Not at *my* age…!"

Rebecca hid a smile and broke into a flood of words, "Emily's working as a guide at a haunted house!" she said and Robin stopped short.

"What? Em, how lucky for you. Are there any handsome ghosts around there? Ha-ha! Oh, God, I'm *so* sorry, I forgot about your husband in Afghanistan." Robin reached across the table and patted Emily's hand. "Tell me all about it, Dear."

Emily had been working at History House for over two months and loved her job, and true to her word avoided talking about ghosts and haunted houses. She was hearing the soft laugh more often now, didn't even bother to check out the footsteps anymore. Added to that, she was hearing bits and pieces of conversations, or, she told herself, she *imagined* she was hearing bits and pieces of conversations. Indeed, the eerie presence was a comfort to her. Since that first evening she'd seen the lonely stranger on the seawall, Emily simply didn't want to share these things with anyone.

She took a sip of her latte and cleared her throat, "It's a really pretty old officer's house on Fort Hancock, way on the north end of Sandy Hook, and it's *not* haunted. I take tourists through the house and keep an eye on things." She stopped a moment. "But, you know something? I'm really getting into all the nineteen-forties lifestyle. Those people seemed to be so much more…well, creative than we are now. We just sit around and log on and off. We can reach anyone, anywhere and…I mean…we can even buy our *groceries* on line, for heaven's sake. I'm beginning to think I'd really rather live back then. It was, well…easier, in some ways…"

Robin looked slightly confused and Rebecca looked concerned. She studied Emily's red lipstick and shoulder-length bob. "Don't let it get to you, Kiddo. They had to contend with the Second World War, not to mention the Great Depression. And rationing! Who would stand for rationing today? Ha! I ask you? That couldn't have been fun and we scream bloody murder now if gas goes up two cents a gallon." She was indignant, "we are so spoiled now, I doubt anyone of us could put up with any of that stuff for five minutes." Emily smiled and the other two women changed the subject.

Later that evening, Emily fixed herself a snack, getting ready to crash in front of the TV. Her mind returned to their conversation and with a box of cheese crackers in her hand and a half-gallon of milk on the counter in front of her, she looked around the kitchen, thinking about the changes she could make on her own.

She dropped onto the sofa with a glass of milk and crackers on a tray, the television turned to another absurd reality show. "Oh, God, how dumb," Emily said to the empty house, and with televised shouts of laugher fading into the background, she began to make a mental list: no washer and dryer means fresh air and sunshine, AC turned *off*, no dishwasher…all can go*!* Emily smiled for the first time in days.

CHAPTER TWENTY-EIGHT

BETTY AND JOYCE

1944

MARY ELLEN BECK, the blissfully adoring wife of Colonel Alexander Beck, slapped her cards down on the table and said, "I'm out!" Mary Ellen lived with her husband and twin teenaged girls in the fanciest house on Officers' Row, a fact she never failed to remind her guests when hosting afternoon teas or card parties. She would bat her eyelashes and lisp, "Rank has its privileges," to anyone close enough to hear, "and the Colonel *is* the Commanding Officer, you know."

Anna, Betty's housekeeper, had told her in confidence that Vivian, Mary Ellen's housekeeper, had told her, in confidence of course, that Colonel Beck sometimes wore his wife's clothes. Betty was scandalized but amused.

"Vivian told me," Anna said in her broken English, "that she come upstairs one afternoon and see him in big bedroom, dressing in long, green dress and black feather thing for neck. He *admiring* himself," she concluded in a shocked voice.

Betty had sworn Anna to silence. "This would cause a terrible scandal in Fort Hancock," she told her, "not to mention in the whole United States Army *at a time of war!*"

Anna agreed she would tell no one else and promised to order Vivian to do the same. Betty decided that she would never even whisper a word of this to James. Nevertheless, now that the cat was out of the bag, when James and Betty were being entertained at the Beck household, she could never look at the colonel without imagining him in Mrs. Beck's emerald green satin evening gown and black feather boa. Oh, Lord, she lamented, how can I ever talk to that man again? She was afraid if she did, he would catch her leering at him, so she was careful to look elsewhere when he was greeting them.

Eight ladies were seated around two card tables set up in Mary Ellen's swank living room, and when Mary Ellen played out, that meant it was time for the rest of them to do so as well, stacking their cards on the tables and chatting while they waited for refreshments to be served. Joyce Stern, Betty's closest friend on Fort Hancock, was sitting across from her. Betty suddenly snorted when she saw Vivian bringing in the tea and cakes, and Joyce glanced at her and raised her eyebrows: *"What?"* Betty would love to tell her friend what she'd heard, but knew she couldn't be part of any gossip in case it did, in fact, get out and cause a scandal *"in a time of war,"* so she smiled back demurely and took a tissue out of her purse and lightly patted her lips.

Betty and Joyce had become friends after one of the afternoon tea parties the year before. They often spent long afternoons in their sailor blouses and shorts, walking along the seawall or sitting on Betty's veranda, drinking Coca-Cola and gossiping: Betty in her soft southern drawl and Joyce in her "down east" folksy accent.

Joyce had been born and raised in Blue Hill, a tiny, picturesque town on the rocky coast of Maine. So, when one day Betty had talked longingly of the warm, blue waters off the coast of North Carolina, Joyce regaled her with tales of the northern Atlantic: so cold one would have to wear bathing slippers to keep their feet from freezing. "You could turn blue in a minute," she told Betty proudly and Betty looked at her in amazement. "Go on," she said, "do people really *like* swimming in Maine?" She shook her head in wonder. *"I* love the Outer Banks." She smiled dreamily. "The water's so warm and soft. At night when you come out, you glow because of the sea algae in the ocean."

Joyce patted Betty's knee. "You're such a hothouse flower, Betty." She laughed her raucous laugh.

As different as the two young women were, they became fast friends very quickly. Joyce was so rowdy that even Della stayed away, another endearing feature as far as Betty was concerned. Joyce lived two doors down from Betty with her husband, Captain Stern, and their three young boys. Bill Stern worked in the same department as James, translating Italian dispatches. The Sterns had been transferred to Fort Hancock the year before Betty and her husband had arrived, and Joyce knew every nook and cranny of the fort. She was more than happy to show Betty the ways of army life on the coast of New Jersey.

Betty recalled an especially comical trip to the PX soon after they'd met. The PX was housed in a brick building and consisted of one huge room with high ceilings crisscrossed by large pipes. It was filled with long wooden counters piled with everything from clothing to housing items. By the front door, five cashiers were kept busy checking out the various and sundry items snapped up by the army wives. A small tearoom with a few tables and chairs was in the back by racks of clothes.

This day, Joyce had spotted a pair of glass candlesticks and was examining one of them when a stout woman wearing a small red hat picked up the other one. "Excuse me, Ma'am," Joyce said sweetly, "that is my candlestick. See? I have the mate right here in my hand."

Red Hat looked at Joyce for a moment, then said, "Sorry, your loss. I want this one."

Joyce looked stunned. "But, they're a *pair!*"

"Gee, your loss. I'm going to buy this one," the woman said sourly and lifted her chin.

Joyce turned to Betty and said in a stage whisper, "She's from *New York,* betcha!" Betty stood by, shocked, speechless.

The woman turned her back, walked stiffly away, the mate to Joyce's glass candlestick clutched to her bosom. Joyce grabbed Betty's hand. "Come on," she whispered and the two women scurried down the next aisle, stalking the rude shopper.

A half-hour later, Joyce and Betty sat dejectedly in the small PX tearoom, each with a cup of tea. As the cashiers began to shut their counters down, Betty spotted the other glass candlestick sitting on a counter. "The candlestick," she whispered and Joyce leapt into action, sweeping it up before Red Hat could change her mind. Every time Betty heard Joyce's raucous laugh, it would remind her of that day in the PX and she would smile all over again.

After tea and cakes were served, Betty and Joyce left Mary Ellen's house together, smiling and waving at the other officers' wives as they turned up Officers' Row. "Joyce," Betty grabbed her friend's hand, "why don't you ask Bill to buy you a bicycle? I love to ride off the fort and down by the beach. It's so lonely and beautiful...in a lonely way, of course. We could have such fun together. Just think."

Joyce gave it some thought; "I suppose I could tell Ol' Bill I'd fetch the groceries...in a little cart...attached to the bicycle. Ha-ha! That way he'd think it would be a good idea." Betty smiled at the thought, and by the time she left Joyce at her house they had a plan how to convince Bill to buy a bicycle for Joyce.

Joyce never had a chance to ask him. When he came home that night, he had new orders with him. Bill was to be sent to London to work with British Intelligence; Joyce and the boys would be moving back to Maine. Two months later they were gone.

After Joyce left Fort Hancock, Betty never found another friend to take her place. When she visited the PX now, she thought it was filled with ghosts.

CHAPTER TWENTY-NINE

CLOTHESPINS

JULY 2009

EMILY GLANCED IN the bathroom mirror, brushed her hair back and made a face. She had decided to spend her time off on Monday making the changes she'd visualized: no dishwasher, no AC, no washer and dryer. After touching up her lipstick she headed downstairs.

She figured this might be an impossible scavenger hunt, but the sweet summer weather and light breezes added to her longing to hang her wash out to dry in the sun instead of throwing the wet load into the dryer. She was determined to find what she wanted. On Thursday evening she'd bought a green plastic dishpan and drainer in Kmart and was washing her dishes every night instead of stacking them in the dishwasher.

Becca called and they'd discussed it. "I want to start hand-washing my laundry and hanging it outside. Does this seem strange to you?" Emily decided to trust her friend's point of view and welcomed her phone call.

Rebecca had become concerned with Emily's peculiar 1940s obsessions, visualized the red lipstick and dated hairstyle. "Well, not that I would consider it *totally* bizarre," she said after a minute, "but don't you have enough to do without draping yourself over the bathtub, hand-scrubbing your laundry and then hauling it out to dry on a clothesline? For heaven's sake, with *clothespins?*

I mean Em, that's so much more work, not to mention damned old-fashioned. Jeesh!"

Emily was determined and finally Becca gave up and made a few suggestions about buying "a clothesline and clothespins, for heaven's sake!" At her kitchen table with her phone in her hand, she rolled her eyes.

Derek was amused when Emily told him her plan. Since arriving in Afghanistan he'd become fit and tan, but more solemn with each video call. Emily was happy she'd made him smile. "Whatever floats your boat, Honey," he said and she rattled on about tomato plants, sun-dried laundry and clotheslines versus washing machines and dryers. After they'd logged off she realized he had had little to say and she stopped short at the kitchen door, her mind going back over what he *had* said, a small frown on her face. After a few minutes she shrugged it off and hurried upstairs to change her clothes and get ready for a day of shopping.

She started with the big box stores, Home Depot and Lowe's, wandering up and down the aisles until young clerks in orange or red smocks would take pity on her and ask what she was looking for. Her request brought puzzled smiles, shrugs and no results.

"Clothesline? Clothespins? Uh…really?

"Thank you, I'll look in Lowe's."

"Ha-ha, maybe my grandmother has some in her attic!"

"Thank you, I'll look…uh…in Ace…"

After three trips she decided to drive into the town center to see if there were any local hardware stores. Parking the car on the shady main street, she headed to Adalet's Apron for coffee and a sweet roll while she studied the people walking up and down the street outside. Atlantic Highlands was a pretty town with flowers along the tree-lined sidewalks and smart stores and boutiques. She enjoyed spending time in the tearoom or window-shopping along the main street and decided to relax for a few minutes before starting her search.

Adalet came over with the coffeepot. "You go shopping?" She filled Emily's cup. "Good day for going out, yes?"

Emily smiled. "Believe it or not, I'm looking for a clothesline and clothespins. The weather is so warm and sunny now, I want to start hanging my laundry out in the fresh air." She blew lightly on her hot coffee.

"I know of store." Adalet sat down across from Emily. "It is down one, or um...two side street from here. It's named Welcome Home and a nice lady owns it for years. I know she helps you." She nodded her head firmly.

"You're kidding, right here in Atlantic Highlands?"

"Right here in Atlantic Highlands, yes." Adalet stood up and headed back to help a teenaged girl who was gazing at sweet cakes in the glass case. "I bet you can find those things in Welcome Home."

Emily finished her coffee and hurried up Main Street, glancing down the side streets as she crossed. Halfway down the third street, she found Welcome Home, the name printed in faded letters on a green awning. Inside, the walls were lined with brass fittings for drawers and cabinet doors: white china handles with smart decorations, tiny flowers or colorful vegetables. An elderly woman, shaped like a ripe pear, smiled at her from behind the counter. "Let me know if I can help you, Dear," she called as Emily passed.

Emily walked up and down the aisles, looking at drawer lining paper, glassware, toasters and coffeepots and, toward the back of the store, a bin filled with twine and balls of string...but no clotheslines and no pins. Frustrated, she walked back to the counter. "Yes, maybe you can help me," she smiled at the Little Pear. "I know this is unusual, but I'm looking for a clothesline and clothespins."

Instead of another apology, she was rewarded with a sweet smile. "I think you can still find those on Ludlow Street on the Lower East Side." The clerk's eyes twinkled. "In Manhattan, you know?" I grew up there and sometimes I go back when I am looking for something, well...*old-fashioned.*"

Emily was delighted. "Thank you so much," she said, suddenly energized. "I honestly didn't think I'd ever find them. Actually, I do know the Lower East Side. My husband and I used to go to Katz's Deli on Delancey Street when we lived in Manhattan. We loved walking around the narrow streets. You know, those fascinating old tenements?"

Laughing, the elderly clerk added, "Ah, yes, Katz's Deli: 'Send a Salami to Your Son in the Army.' World War Two. Back when I was a kid, I lived in one of those tenements." Her face took on a far-away expression.

Emily imagined the Little Pear as a "kid" and headed home, anxious and eager for her trip to the City. It never occurred to her that this was an odd compulsion or that her friend Rebecca was becoming more and more concerned.

CHAPTER THIRTY

NEW YORK CITY

JULY 2009

LIBERTY STATE PARK sprawls along the New Jersey side of the Hudson River and faces Manhattan. The summer before the World Trade Center disaster, Emily and Derek had often driven north to the park to spend the day. They'd walk along a path rimmed by gorse and blackberry thickets, past the Interpretive Wild Bird Center, tucked into it's little grove of trees and along the canal where the sailboats and motor yachts nose into the piers. On warm summer Saturdays they would sit on a grassy hill overlooking one of the big open fields, watching as the children sent their kites spinning and swirling into the sky. At the end of the day, they'd walk along the canal to the Lightship, a café long since closed, joining the sailing crowd with their open shirts and loafered feet and when the sun set, the twin towers across the river would glow with pink light, reflecting back the western sky. Emily and Derek would share sandwiches and glasses of wine, watching the bright yellow water taxi as it moved back and forth from the Liberty State Park dock to midtown Manhattan. Before dark, they'd find their way back to the Honda and head home.

Now the towers were gone and each September two white beams of light would shine from the empty space, reaching into the night sky. People would be a little bit quieter. Someday soon a new tower would be built to fill the space.

Emily decided to take off the following Friday and wheedled a reluctant John Rogers into babysitting History House while she was gone. Much as he disliked the idea, he agreed, shuddering as he hung up the phone.

The New York ferryboat to lower Manhattan left from Hoboken, a New Jersey river town near Liberty State Park, and there was a light rail that would take her from the park to Hoboken. She could park in the lot next to the train station. She hadn't been back since the Lightship had closed and felt a stir of excitement as she turned her car north on the parkway early Friday morning. Summer was bringing people to the Jersey shore towns for vacation and the parkway heading south was bumper to bumper, inching painfully along: boats in tow, back seats stuffed with belongings, children, dogs, heading south a day early. Emily turned the car radio to a local music station and relaxed, enjoying the trip. Much more fun than the ferryboat from Atlantic Highlands, she thought. An adventure.

Soon the scrub pines disappeared and tall green trees lined the highway, motels and business buildings hiding here and there among the foliage. She turned toward Manhattan and passed Newark's Liberty Airport and could see the City in the distance. At the tollbooth she paid and turned off at the Liberty State Park exit, winding her way down into the parking lot. One of the light-rail trains was pulling out of the station as she locked her car door.

"Plenty more where that came from," a young man shouted as he ran past."

Emily stopped by the ticket machine. "The best way to travel," she commented to a woman standing behind her. She collected her ticket, found a bench and by the time the next Hoboken-bound train pulled in, was checking the NYC ferry schedule.

The light rail pulled out of the station and headed for its next stop. Emily could see the ancient cobbled road that cut through the park and down to the river. A few cars were bumping over its uneven surface. The little café was gone, but she could see the big *Lightship*, its namesake, moored next to the water taxi. Briefly, she saw the yacht basin with the sleek cruisers and sailboats lined up along the piers. The gentle toot of a horn in the distance announced the arrival of the Liberty water taxi, and then the train was past Liberty State Park.

Emily gathered her belongings at the Hoboken Station and followed the others into the big railroad station, hurried past the New Jersey Transit rail lines and into the ferry terminal. The 1:00 p.m. ferry was just pulling into its slip as she bought her ticket, and she joined the tourists climbing the ramp to the walkway, stepping carefully down the gangplank's swaying boards.

The view of the City was wonderful. Emily stood on the deck and drank in the sight as the ferry plowed across the Hudson River. They skirted the space where the twin towers had stood and pulled into the dock at Battery Park City and the financial district. Some of the passengers disembarked; the ferry gave a cheerful blast of the horn and pulled out again, rounding the end of Manhattan and heading into the East River. Emily breathed the warm air and hummed softly. At Pier 11 she got off and, after looking around for a minute, headed away from the river and toward the city.

At South Street Seaport, the big Pier 17 building jutted out into the water like the prow of an ancient seafaring vessel. Emily loved Pier 17 with its shops and pubs, and the night before she'd called Barbara Hunt, a good friend and author from her days working at *Around the City*. The two planned to meet at one of the pubs that evening, and as she stood gazing at the City, she suddenly longed to see her coworkers again. Her heart skipped a beat and she took a quick skip as she crossed the street, turned north and thought: It's been too long to be without my friends.

Emily walked slowly up the East Side, looking into store windows and pausing at one of the small pocket parks that dotted Manhattan. At Delancey Street, she turned into the warren of small streets and alleys that made up the Lower East Side.

This area of New York City has been home to millions of emigrants over the years: Irish, escaping the potato famine in the 1840s; Germans who left their homes following the Revolution of 1848; and Eastern Europeans, making it the homeland for American immigrant Jews. It is a crowded, vibrant area of the City but the era of crowded tenements and teeming streets is long gone; the Lower East Side has become gentrified with quaint boutiques and restaurants. Still, it holds a certain charm and Emily loved to walk through the narrow streets.

She reached Ludlow Street, turned the corner and stopped short. In front of her was a small, grubby variety store with big windows and a sign declaring: *You Can Find Anything Here!* A smaller sign, hanging precariously off the door, announced: *If you can't find it in here, it doesn't exist.* Emily swung her bag over her shoulder and opened the door.

A bell tinkled as she entered and a man, tall and thin like a long-legged waterbird, pushed aside a curtain in the back and came to greet her. Emily looked around hopefully. She was standing in the narrowest room she had ever seen. It reminded her of a dusty old subway car; everything but the kitchen sink was hanging off the walls and stacked on shelves behind the counter.

The clerk matched his store. He had a narrow face, a complexion as gray as day-old ashes and was worrying a toothpick in one of his front teeth. His head was balanced on a long neck that stuck out of a collar a size too large. Thin wrists and narrow hands hung out of the sleeves of a worn black jacket. A heavy chain holding keys and a silver bottle opener hung from his belt.

"Good afternoon, Miss, I'm Mr. Marchetti." He tossed the toothpick under the counter. "We have every single thing you have ever wanted in your young life, right here in this store."

Emily cringed as the toothpick disappeared and hoped there was a wastebasket under the counter. She gave him her best smile and launched into her story: "…hanging laundry outside in the sun, clotheslines and clothespins, no big stores have such things anymore. So," she concluded, "I've been looking everywhere. The woman who owns Welcome Home down in South Jersey, where I live, told me about Ludlow Street. She…uh…grew up here…" She looked expectantly at Mr. Marchetti.

"Yeah," he said shortly, as he stalked toward the back of the store. "Here ya go, Little Lady." He slipped a plastic wrapped clothesline off a hook on the wall, looked under the counter for a minute. "Aha…" He straightened up and plopped the clothesline and a package of wooden clothespins on the counter.

"Awesome!" Emily was impressed.

Seeing this, Mr. Marchetti brightened up. "Told ya, Little Lady, anything you ever wanted, right here in this old store," he showed yellow teeth in a wide smile.

She handed him a twenty-dollar bill and he turned to an antique upright cash register, banging a few keys until a drawer sprang out with a clang. Emily pocketed her change while Mr. Marchetti bundled her purchases in brown paper and green twine, tying the twine up in a fancy bow.

"Here ya go, Little Lady." He handed her the package. "Enjoy your day!" He found another toothpick in his jacket pocket, popped it into his mouth and headed back to the curtained door. A sudden burst of canned TV laughter carried into the dusty, narrow shop.

CHAPTER THIRTY-ONE

THE FÜHRER IS DEAD

1945

O N MONDAY, APRIL 30, James came home early from his office and Betty's heart jumped with alarm. A few weeks earlier, he'd arrived before the end of the day and, grim-faced, he'd taken her hand in both of his and gently told her that President Roosevelt had died from a stroke the day before, then held her close as she sobbed in his arms. This time he had a bunch of wilting wildflowers in his hand and a big smile on his face and Betty relaxed.

"Adolf Hitler just committed suicide. He married his gal friend, Eva Braun, and then they shot themselves in his bunker underneath Berlin." He hugged Betty and danced her around the kitchen.

The army wives had been following as much of the latest news as they could on their living-room radios and knew things were changing in Europe, but Betty was still shocked at the news.

"Hitler…shot himself? How can this be?"

"I guess he knew he was finished when the Yanks came to town." James dropped down into one of the kitchen chairs and leaned back with his hands behind his head.

"Dead!" Betty's heart started beating fast.

James slammed the chair forward. "I know it'll be a weeknight, but can you get Anna to babysit next Monday night? I'll be able to get away by then and I want to take *my* best gal to New York City!" He blew her a kiss and leaned back again and smiled. "Can you call Anna and make sure she can babysit?"

Betty nodded and hurried to the phone. She dialed the main telephone dispatch and when the base operator finally answered, gave him Anna's phone number on the mainland, her heart pounding.

"Hitler's dead." She whispered into the phone when she heard Anna's voice. "Hitler's dead, Anna." For a minute, there was silence on the other end; then Betty heard bitter sobs, a sniff, and more sobs over the miles, and she knew Anna was absorbing the news: the end to her nightmare. She waited patiently and finally Anna's voice came over the phone.

"Thank you, Mrs. Betty. I'm sorry to cry so, but it is a miracle. It will end now, I think, the war."

Betty hesitated then continued, "James wants to take me out to celebrate Monday night." She held her breath. "Can you babysit? Will this be okay?"

"I will be very happy to babysit while you celebrate, Mrs. Betty. Of course I will come out and stay for you." Anna blew her nose and Betty heard a soft laugh over the phone.

The next day Joseph Goebbels, the Minister of Propaganda and just-named Hitler successor, joined him. He and his wife, Magda, killed their six children and committed suicide together.

Betty turned off the radio and called Anna to let her know this latest news. "Oh, dear, as relieved as I am that the war in Europe is finally coming to an end, the idea of people shooting themselves or hanging themselves, killing their children, jumping out of windows, whatever…it seems barbaric. It makes me sick." Betty shook her head in disbelief.

"No me," Anna said in a firm voice, "Maybe now Hell ends in the world. Maybe we all go home again." That ended the conversation.

The continued surprising news from Europe couldn't dim Betty's excitement about the trip to New York City, and when Monday evening arrived she dressed in her best outfit: a soft lavender dress with white roses across a full skirt, white peep-toed sandals with wedge heels and a small, jaunty hat with a veil that covered her eyes.

Anna came to Fort Hancock early and put the children to bed while Betty dressed, singing softly to Bobbie before she turned off the light. When Betty came downstairs, Anna was sitting in the kitchen with James, coffee cups on the table in front of them.

James smiled his wide smile and jumped up when Betty came into the hallway. "Honey, you look just *swell!*" He put his arm around her and looked back at Anna. "Wow! Just look at my pretty housewife, she looks like a model from Vogue magazine. I'll be honored to escort her to New York City tonight."

Anna clapped her hands, laughing, as Betty spun around in front of them, showing off her outfit. "Beautiful Lady. She goes to celebrate such good news." Anna followed them into the back hall, watched as they left, carefully locked the back door and, smiling, headed back to the kitchen to wash the cups and clean off the table. All is well in the world, she thought, and it's about time!

CHAPTER THIRTY-TWO

EMILY AND BARBARA

JULY 2009

AFTER LEAVING MR. Everything-You-Ever-Wanted, Emily walked up to the next street for lunch and some window-shopping. Orchard Street was famous for fashions at discount prices and she had the afternoon to browse. Stopping at an ancient coffee shop on the corner of Orchard and Delancey Street, she peered through the window at a narrow room with a long counter running the length of the room. A man in a white paper cap was turning hot dogs on a grill.

Emily slid onto a stool and waited for White Hat to finish with the grill, ordered coffee and a tuna sandwich with a half sour pickle on the side. She sat at the counter and absentmindedly read the signs hanging on the back wall: *Delicious Hebrew Kosher Franks, Kosher Meals, Dr. Brown's Cream Soda, Rest Rooms for Customers only–that means You! No Smoking!*

"More coffee, Miss?" The counterman was holding the coffeepot over her cup, his eyebrows raised. She blinked and shook her head, looked back through the window, feeling as if she had just awakened from a dream. Oh, God, I miss Derek so much, she thought, a hard lump in her throat. I'm so lonely. Wistfully she picked up her sandwich and looked at it. This was our city: Little Italy for dinner, Chinatown for Sunday dim sum, Central Park in the spring. What am I doing here alone? She sighed, brushed crumbs off her lap. Shrugging, she popped the last bite of sandwich into her mouth and turned away from the window.

Emily arrived at Pier 17 a few minutes before six and found a seat on one of the benches that had sprung up like mushrooms around the large outdoor deck. She sat quietly, gazing at the *Peking*, an antique four-masted schooner that had been moored in South Street Seaport for decades and the subject of one of her first articles for *Around the City*

The *Peking*, one of the last generations of windjammers, launched in Germany in 1911 and used in the nitrate and grain trade, sailing to South America and around the dangerous Cape Horn. In 1975, the Seaport museum had acquired the long-retired *Peking* and towed her to her current home at Pier 16, restoring her to early grandeur in the 1990s. Now here she sat, in all her glory, safe and snug in New York Harbor, entertaining tourists from around the world.

The evening was warm and Emily felt happy as she sat looking out at the East River and the lovely old ship. Good old *Peking*, she said, breathing in the warm air. I'm glad to see you again. She could still smell the faint odor of fish from the Fulton Fish Market, an old and smelly open-air market that had been relocated four years earlier. As the sun sank behind the Manhattan buildings, the breeze ruffled her hair and Emily felt at peace with the world, her sorrow at lunch forgotten.

A little after six o'clock she heard her name called from across South Street and saw Barbara and two other old friends holding up traffic as they trooped across the street.

Emily smiled and leaned back in her barrel chair, wiping her lips on a napkin. The four women had found a cozy pub in Pier 17 and polished off a large pepperoni pizza. Barbara Hunt had been Emily's office mate and cowriter for the five years she had worked at *Around the City*. The two young editors had spent hours visiting old buildings and remote locations all through New York City and filled their articles with interesting insights and strange tidbits that captivated their readers.

Four years earlier Barbara divorced her husband after finding him carousing in their bedroom with the Ecuadorian housekeeper and Emily was her shoulder to cry on during that dark and painful winter. The experience brought them closer than mere coworkers and Emily suddenly realized how much she missed her friend.

Barbara had bounced back and was telling Emily about Rolf, her new boyfriend. "Wonderful man, just wonderful," she said, beaming.

Red-headed Carole Barnes was *Around the City*'s manufacturing director, and Deb Chase, a slim, sweet-faced woman, was art director. The four women had worked together and had often gone out for dinner after work. As usual, Barbara and Emily shared the conversation and the other two settled into their own world of design files and paper versus electronic delivery systems. Barbara signaled the waiter and ordered another carafe of wine and Emily told them about her job at History House.

Again, she found herself reluctant to say too much and only offered a cursory summary. "It's pretty out there on Sandy Hook." She sipped her wine. "The house is very big and very old and I have at least a dozen tourists in and out every day." She paused and realized it was pretty boring. Actually, she had to admit, hideously dull. "I like it," she ended lamely.

Barbara seemed engaged, but Carol and Deb had lost interest and were chatting between themselves. It reminded Emily of the days she had spent with these friends, hobnobbing with Barbara while the other two dithered over "files or printers errors, typefaces and column measurements" and even now, seated at Pier 17, Emily heard from their corner: "Awful design, not a good suggestion," "…too much saturation in the art…" It was familiar and made her smile.

The waiter brought their wine and topped off each glass before placing the carafe in front of Emily. Barbara sat forward in her chair with her elbows on the table.

"Em," her voice was suddenly serious, "why don't you come back to *Around the City*? Jonesy would hire you back in a minute, even as a freelance editor. He always loved your writing and I could sure use your creative insight. My God, it's so insufferably boring with you gone!"

Emily smiled and raised an eyebrow. "I *was* pretty good, wasn't I?" she laughed. "I might just give it some thought."

"Design solution...," Deb said to Carole in their private conversation.

"Look, Em," Barbara continued, "why don't you call Jonesy? Tell him that you're working now, but certainly they'll be closing that house in September. You could start in October. What d'ya say?"

Emily's smile froze. Close the house! She was stunned. In all the time she'd been working there, over four whole months, she'd never thought about the house being closed, not once, and the last month she'd conveniently forgotten this was only a temporary job.

Barbara touched her hand. "Are you OK, Em? You look like you've seen a ghost." She searched her face.

Emily felt her eyes fill with tears and picked up her glass. "I think I'm just tired and I worry about Derek," she said and excused herself, putting the glass back down again. "Just let me run to the Ladies for a few minutes. I'll be fine."

She washed her face with cool water and stared at her image in the mirror. Her eyes were dull and her face pale, all the laughter and joy gone. She smoothed her hair, pinched her cheeks to regain a little color and headed back to the table. Shortly afterward she gave Barbara a hug and a promise to call *Around the City's* executive editor, waved at Carole and Deb and headed down to the Pier 11 ferry terminal.

As she sat in the ferry, with the lights of Manhattan spread out behind her, and later heading down the Garden State Parkway, all she could hear was, "close the house, close the house," and she felt as though her heart would break.

CHAPTER THIRTY-THREE

NEW YORK CITY

1945

J AMES AND BETTY took the Fort Hancock ferry to New York City. It made two round-trip crossings with a stop at the New Jersey Central Railroad Terminal in Jersey City, one trip in the morning and one at night, and arrived in downtown Manhattan at seven o'clock that evening and returned to Fort Hancock at eleven p.m.

Anna would stay in one of the big third-floor guest rooms that night. "You won't have to worry about making a late trip home, Anna, and the upstairs guest room is very comfortable," Betty told her on the phone. Anna brought an overnight kit with her nightie and toothbrush.

The weather was cool and blustery onboard the ferryboat. James and Betty stayed inside, looking out at the dark sea and busy waves. As the first dim lights of the City came into view, Betty's heart raced. During their whole stay in New Jersey, she'd never been to Manhattan. After the long war years and blackouts some of the lights had only recently been lit at night. "James, this is such an adventure." Betty grabbed his arm in excitement, peered out as the city came closer.

The ferry wound its way across the water and Betty could see the battleships that prowled New York Harbor, sitting low in the water; overhead a pale dirigible hung in the sky like a strange airborne sea monster. James took her hand and smiled down at her, scanned the skyline. "Someday soon all the lights will be turned on. New York City will be the city of lights again." He softly added, "Then we can all go home." It was the same thing that Anna had said.

Home, Betty smiled to herself. Home to the lavender mountains of Asheville...or maybe the rolling ocean waves of the Outer Banks of North Carolina. She gazed at James, his face turned to the city, and her heart skipped a beat. Just like I'm sixteen years old, again, she thought.

When the ferry docked in downtown Manhattan, they got off with the other passengers and hurried to the nearest subway station. "I'm taking my best gal somewhere special," he told the uniformed woman in the tollbooth. He handed her two shiny nickels. When they descended the steps into the station, Betty looked around anxiously.

There were people standing on the platform. Oh dear, New York City people, Betty thought and it made her uneasy. Everyone seemed to be celebrating and a man standing next to them suddenly burst into song, rousing and off-key but heartfelt: *Shine on, shine on harvest moon up in the sky...la la la*. James laughed and joined in and by the time the subway train pulled in, everyone was singing, *You're a grand old flag, you're a high flying flag...la la la di da...* and Betty was singing along.

They found seats in the first section of the train and Betty looked around with interest. Benches ran along both sides of the subway car and were made of straw, looked like straw and smelled like straw. She sniffed and decided she liked the smell. "This reminds me of home in the summer." She took a deep breath. "Straw, grass, farms, country...hmm."

James inhaled, laughed: "Straw, grass, country bumpkins!"

"Hey!" Betty slapped his hand, "not country bumpkins. County pumpkins in the fall and country corn and sweet melons in the summer."

At their stop James pulled her out of her seat and they dashed up the steps into City Hall Park. Betty stopped and looked around, her eyes wide. "Gee, look at this! How big and how exciting and...all the people are out *celebrating.*" She decided then and there that this would be another of her "most wonderful days." Even if it's night now, she added.

James took her hand as they strolled toward City Hall. At the restaurant, he opened the door and gallantly ushered her into a large and dazzling dining room: red, black, gold and yellow repeating itself in the wallpaper, the tables and even the chairs, the walls covered with mirrors and murals, the large room filled with dramatic lighting.

"And, here we are," he watched as her eyes widened. "Does this suit Madam?"

A maître'd, wearing a black tuxedo and bowtie, showed them to a large round banquette and handed them red, yellow and gold menus with the name *Longchamps* in dark red scripted letters on the front. Betty was spellbound. "Look at these menus!" She opened it up and gasped. "Look at these *prices!* Breaded Veal Cutlets, $1.45! And look," she scanned the page, "Whole Broiled Lobster, $2.75. Wow!"

James lifted her hand and lightly kissed the palm. "Just get what you want, Honey, it's a celebration. History is being made right at this very minute!" He patted it and let it go as a waiter, dressed in a white jacket and red-and-gold bowtie, arrived with water and a basket with bread and a small crock of butter nestled in a crisp white napkin.

"And *butter!*" Betty stared. "Real butter? This isn't oleomargarine?"

James turned to the waiter. "Bring us each a glass of your best wine and we'll both have the lobster." He winked at Betty, "Ritzy, huh?"

When James and Betty came home that night, she dropped her bag on the dining-room table and gave him a hug. "This has been one of the best nights of my life: the ferry ride, the City, the beautiful Longchamps *and* the wine and lobster, oh, and the *butter!*" Exhausted but happy, she climbed the stairs.

James disappeared into his study again and closed the door. It was close to two o'clock in the morning when they fell asleep.

At two forty-one a.m. on the morning of Tuesday, May 7, the German Armed Forces High Command, General Alfred Jodl, signed the unconditional surrender documents for all German forces to the Allies.

In Norway, General Franz Böhme announced the surrender of German troops the same day. It included the phrase: "All forces under German control to cease active operations at twenty-three hundred and one hours Central European Time on May eight, nineteen forty-five."

That May morning Americans awoke to the news that World War II was over in Europe and that May 8 was to be declared V-E Day. Everyone cheered and hugged each other. Strangers shouted, sang in the streets; Americans danced and kissed one another and wept in relief across the country. Betty brought the children to the parade ground to see Fort Hancock's celebrations. She sat with the other wives and they talked in low, excited voices.

"What does this mean?"

"Warren says the war will end soon."

"But when, when?"

"Well, he says soon, but not when. I wish he would say more but he doesn't want to worry the children."

"And what about Japan?"

"He won't say. What does James say, Betty?"

"He doesn't say, just listens to the new every night."

While they gossiped, the children raced around, roughhousing and rolling in the grass shouting: "Patooey patooey in the Führer's face! Hitler is dead, Hitler is dead!"

The War in Europe had come to an end and the following week Betty received a Liberty Airmail letter from Joyce in Maine.

She carefully opened the delicate envelope and spread the letter out on the kitchen table. Joyce had written in her typical fashion, signing her letter in looping script that was so familiar to Betty. She read:

May 9, 1945

Hello, Hello, Hello,

Because of V-E day, Bill is being returned to Fort Hancock by the end of June and so are we. Yippee! I can't wait to see you and I have sooooo much to tell you. Maine is swell, but I miss good old Fort Hancock, ha-ha-ha! Really, I'll be glad to get back.

Your Best Friend,
Joyce

P.S. I broke my glass candlesticks. Pooh! I'll give you the one that's left. Hey, what's a friend for.

Betty read the words in Joyce's elegant handwriting and felt her heart jump. "So much good news in one week," she told James when he came home that evening. "The War in Europe has ended, the Sterns are coming back to Fort Hancock and we had a celebration in New York City!" But the war in the Pacific still raged on.

CHAPTER THIRTY-FOUR

A MESSAGE FROM DEREK

JULY 2009

EMILY BEGAN SPENDING more time at History House and less time at home. The last Wednesday in July was muggy and uncomfortable. She logged on to her computer as soon as she got up so her email could download while she showered and dressed. When she came downstairs, she quickly scanned a single message, then read it again more carefully:

> Hi Honey,
>
> I'll be video calling you this evening around 8 p.m. your time. Please make sure you're home. Important!
>
> I love you,
> Derek

The email stunned her. They'd become comfortable with their Saturday evening video calls, catching up on news from home, his life in the Middle East. Derek's email request was alarming; she didn't know what to think about it.

She stopped for her morning coffee, lost in thought, hardly glancing at her friendly counterman. "So, what can I get you today, Pretty Lady?" He gave her a broad smile, then looked at her with concern as he handed her the container. "Are you OK?"

"Thank you, uh…yeah, sure…have a good day." She gave a half-hearted wave and headed out the door. All the way to Sandy Hook she thought about the message and her stomach ached with tension.

What, Derek? What's happened? Are you OK? Should I be worried? What? What? *What?* She pulled into her parking spot outside History House and speed-dialed Becca's number. "Be home, Becca, please, please be home!" The phone rang three times and then her friend's cheerful voice came on the answering machine: "Wades here, or in this case, *not*! Please leave us a message. Thank yoooo!"

Damn! Emily left a short, tense message, climbed out of the car, balancing the coffee cup while she slung her pocketbook over her shoulder. She dropped her bag on the desk and took the cup into the kitchen, tossing the remains down the drain. As she measured fresh coffee into the percolator she began to calm down. By the time she'd finished opening the windows and turning on the fans, her fears had faded. I'm sure everything is fine. Of *course* it's fine. Thank you, House, she whispered. You're my refuge.

She settled down in her office and twenty minutes later her cell phone chirped; Becca's soothing voice assured her there was, "of course, nothing to be worried about." "Look, Em," she said, her voice serious. "We have to trust the guys. Let them take care of themselves. I haven't heard a peep from Roger and if he isn't calling, then there's nothing to be alarmed about."

Emily leaned back in her chair and propped a foot on the desk. "Yeah," she said and twirled a pen around her fingers, "I guess I stopped worrying about an hour ago. It's just that Derek and I video call on Saturdays and this is unusual. It's not our schedule, you know?"

The two friends chatted for a few more minutes and promised to meet for dinner one night soon. When they hung up, Emily put her pen down and went to greet a family of tourists who were waiting anxiously at the back door. By the time the family had left, she was busy with a carton of new folders and forgot the video call for the rest of the day.

It had turned out to be hot and sultry and not a breath of air stirred; even the cicadas were quiet. By early afternoon only a few more visitors arrived, took a look and mumbled a quick good-bye. At a little past four o'clock, Emily said forget it and decided to close the house for the day and head home.

As she locked the front door, she saw the familiar figure standing on the seawall, staring out over the bay. As usual the young woman was lost in thought, her dark hair ruffled by the warm breeze that had started drifting across the bay. Emily watched for a minute and then shivered. Oh, damn! Now I'm beginning to get superstitious! Stop it, Emily…Stop it!

She hurriedly locked the door, finished closing up the rest of the house and headed home; but as she inched down Hartshorne Drive in the summer traffic her mind returned to Derek's video call and the woman on the seawall faded into the background. Not bothering to stop for groceries, she pulled into the driveway and hurried into the house, grabbing the mail as she came through the door.

She dropped her pocketbook and the mail on the kitchen table and raced upstairs to change, dumping her work clothes on the floor, then slumped on the bed and put her head in her hands. Six-thirty. Only six-thirty and now I have to wait for an hour and a half. My God, I feel like I'm living in a nightmare. Emily coughed out a dry sob and a few hot tears burned her eyes. Oh, Lord! She rubbed her face hard with both hands. I can't even cry anymore.

After a few minutes she went downstairs and made herself a cup of tea and sat at the kitchen table, staring at the computer's blank face as the minutes ticked by, her stomach balled into a tight knot. At a little after eight, Emily's computer made a little "bing" and Derek's face appeared. After a few minutes of small talk, he quickly came to the point. "Honey, I won't be able to get in touch with you for a few weeks." His face faded in and out and then stabilized.

Emily felt her heart sink and broke in, "What, why? What's happened?"

"Hey, Honey, don't panic. My unit's headed up into the mountains for a while and I really don't know when we'll be back." He smiled wistfully and continued. "I'll try to get in touch with you when I can, promise, but now I want you to do something for me. It's nothing to be worried about but…uh…remember the file with my will and military papers, all the stuff I brought home?"

Emily nodded. "What about them?"

"Please go into the top drawer in my desk and take it out. Put it on the desk. I want to make sure you have it handy. You know?"

Emily was scared and she knew her face showed it over the thousands of cyber-miles. "Why?" Her voice shook.

"Look, Em, this is just standard procedure. Honest. It's not a dangerous mission, but whenever we go on maneuvers or away from camp we have to tell our families take care of important papers. Please, Honey, don't be worried. Just think of me with happy thoughts and go on about your business. Go do your officer's house business and try to be happy. Try not to worry. It will make it easier for me if you do that."

Emily swallowed hard. "I promise," she said, but her heart felt like it had turned to stone and was sitting somewhere in her lower abdomen. They chatted for a few more awkward minutes before he blew her a kiss and signed off. As his face disappeared, she said softly, "I love you, Derek, I love you." But he was gone.

Shortly after Derek's video call, Emily stopped paying the bills. She'd drive home in the summer traffic, lost in thought, and when she got home, pick up the mail as she came through the front door, look at it, toss it on the pile on the kitchen table and think:

Damn the mail. Nothing but bills! It's just too much trouble and I can't be bothered. I'm too tired. I'm too damn tired.

Becca called to commiserate: "Roger got in touch with me right after you talked to Derek," she told Emily glumly. "I don't like it either. I really don't feel that terrific, you know, what with being sick every morning and falling asleep unexpectedly. And to top that off, Laura Alexander told me she thought I was too *old* to be having another baby. 'My word,' she said to me, 'just look at you, Rebecca Wade. And at your age!' Can you beat that? And now I have to worry about Roger. Damn!" Rebecca's snort turned into a sob. "It's all so unfair. It just sucks!" She took a breath and sniffed loudly. "So, when are *we* going to get together? You are the only normal person I know and you're busy now with that creepy old house. "

Emily managed to laugh. "I don't know how normal I am anymore, Becca." But she glanced at the calendar hanging by the refrigerator. Any night is ok with me. What's a good time for you?"

"Normal is as normal does, Em…Friday?"

They made plans for dinner the following Friday but Emily promptly forgot it.

CHAPTER THIRTY-FIVE

EMILY

JULY 2009

EVERY DAY THE pile of bills grew and Emily just turned her
back and checked the refrigerator. Hmm, what to eat? What
to eat?

She had stopped shopping and now there was little in the
way of food in the house: frozen biscuits in the freezer, some
cheese in the snack drawer and a few pieces of stale bread in the
breadbox. There were boxes of pasta and rice in the cupboard, and
one evening Emily unearthed an old chocolate Santa that had
been left over from Christmas. She studied it for a few minutes,
and then popped it in her mouth. It was gone in three bites.

She picked ripe tomatoes in her little garden and made
sandwiches with toasted stale bread, boiled pasta and sliced the
cheese into it while it was still hot. Boy, she thought, I'm losing
it. But she'd lost interest in shopping.

The last week of July, Jena called. "Okay, so where are you?
We're still going to yoga, you know. And we're still going to
Adalet's. We miss you. Adalet misses you. We want to hear more
about that officer's house and the ghost or whatever she is."

Emily felt guilty, realized she missed her friends and the
weekly yoga classes. "I just don't seem to feel like going out," she
admitted. "Now that Derek's out there somewhere, God-knows-
where, I don't even know where. I guess I'm just worried."

Until she heard Jena's voice, Emily hadn't thought about yoga at all and was surprised that she'd been missed. "I'm so busy." She sighed, sent Jena a phone kiss and hung up. She sat by the phone for a few minutes and realized that she resented Jena's saying "*that* officer's house." I just don't want to talk about it, she decided, and put Jena out of her mind.

Every morning she jumped out of bed, showered and dressed quickly. She felt more comfortable at History House now, and she didn't waste time at home. Little by little her home began to show her indifference. Dust settled under the bed and brown rust rimmed the bottom of the shower; damp towels were piled in the corner of the upstairs bath. There was no toilet paper in the downstairs bathroom and dishes started filling up in the sink.

One evening Emily came through the back door, stopped and looked around in shock. Oh, my God, what have I done to my poor house? This is *so* bad. I have to do something about this right now! She dropped onto the couch and put her head in her hands, thought: What would Derek say if he could see me now? What's happening to me? She felt as though the strength was being sapped from her body, as if she were sleepwalking through each day. The only place I feel alive is at the officer's house, she said with a sigh.

Stop, Emily, she told herself firmly. Enough of this! Tomorrow I get this house cleaned up before I leave, even if I have to get up at five o'clock in the morning. With this in mind, she went to bed early and slept soundly all night.

The next morning, true to her word, she was up at dawn. She ran soapy water in the sink, scrubbed the dirty dishes and stuck them in the drainer, dusted the living room, washed the sheets in the tub and hung them out on the line, where they billowed like sails. Then forgot they were there.

What's wrong with me? Emily wondered later, as she sat in her kitchen with a piece of stale toast and a cup of tea. Am I so involved with History House I have no time for my own home?

The thought made her sad, but she brushed it aside, left the empty cup in the sink and dashed out to her car, heading back out to Fort Hancock.

At the end of the month, John Rogers brought Emily her paycheck. "Hey, Kiddo!" The screen door slammed behind him. "Wow!" He shouted as he looked around. "You have this old place looking like new!" He walked through the kitchen and into the front rooms. "Nice!" he said.

Emily followed him out to the veranda. "John, do you have any idea if someone else is living out here? On Fort Hancock, I mean?"

He glanced over at Emily as she joined him on the veranda. "Nope, not that I know of, at least. Why?"

Emily touched his arm. "Every now and then I see a young woman out on the seawall. She always stands there looking out at the bay. Not that I believe in ghosts…ha-ha…but, you know, I really wonder who she is, and I don't feel comfortable bothering her. She seems so…um…preoccupied."

John Rogers smiled and headed back into the house. "I really don't think you have to worry about a ghost, Em, but I have no idea who that could be. Probably one of those bird-watching people that come out to the other house, Number 30, now and then. I know *I've* never seen her."

He dropped her check on the kitchen table and headed out the back door. "See you in a couple of weeks, Kiddo," he called back. "Take care of yourself; don't make friends with any ghosts! Ha-ha-ha!" He climbed into his car and headed back down the dusty street, tooting "bap ba bap" gaily on the horn, but he was frowning again and thought: what's going on?

Emily picked up her check, put it in her pocketbook, then promptly forgot to take it to the bank.

CHAPTER THIRTY-SIX

SHOREBIRDS

1944-1945

BETTY WHEELED HER bicycle away from the garage and headed for the front gate. Her mind was filled with the whispers she was still hearing at the Officers' Club, rumors of the new American weapon: huge and deadly. Something they called atomic. The continuing war in the Pacific was beginning to make her physically ill and now as she pedaled toward the shore, she murmured to herself, "sick and tired, sick and tired!"

Riding her bicycle along the tidal basins and scrub outside Fort Hancock was Betty's great escape. She'd borrowed James' binoculars and carried them in the basket, stopping along the dirt paths, sitting quietly in the brush, waiting for the swallows to fly in from the gun batteries that faced the ocean.

Sometimes, one or two of the elegant great blue herons would wade near the shore of the bay and she could study them through the glasses. She especially loved the cormorants: strange dark waterbirds that dove under the water to search for fish, bursting up with a splash and swimming with just their heads above water. She often saw one of them drying his wide, dark wings in the sun, his snakelike neck curved over his breast.

She started bringing sandwiches and sweet tea in a thermos, spending hours sitting on the seawall, eating lunch and enjoying the wildness of Sandy Hook and the bay. In the fall, the small brant geese arrived, and beautiful black-and-white bufflehead ducks would follow. By October, snow buntings would fly in from the tundra. She would see large flocks of them on the dunes and along the shore, fluttering to the ground like snowflakes. Betty would bundle up in a warm sweater and scarf and pedal out to watch the geese and ducks bobbing on the bay or the buntings swarming among the sea grasses.

She was spending the long war years wandering the shores of Sandy Hook and it brought her peace. Sometimes she would curl up in James' lap and tell him about her day as he stroked the hair back from her face. "The bufflehead ducks are back, James, and they are so elegant with their black and white feathers." Or, "I saw so many buntings it looked like there was a snow storm on the beach."

James would smile and hold her close; but she longed to find someone who could tell her things would be all right.

CHAPTER THIRTY-SEVEN

THE HOUSE AT NUMBER 30

AUGUST 2009

REBECCA WADE TURNED her car into the parking lot behind Antonio's and scanned the parked cars to see if Emily was already there. She *had* called her the night before and left a message reminding her of their dinner, had suggested a nice Italian meal at one of their favorite restaurants and confirmed a seven o'clock seating.

She locked her car and walked across to the portico and through the big ornate doors into Antonio's comfortable dining room. Rebecca was looking forward to seeing Emily, to finding out how her friend was doing with her job and her concern about Derek. Rebecca hadn't heard a word from her husband, either, since the unit had moved into the mountains and was beginning to feel anxious; she imagined Emily was feeling the same way. Their dinner was a welcome escape from her boisterous brood and she was delighted that her housekeeper, Bianca, had been willing to babysit for the evening.

Antonio greeted her and showed her to a cozy booth with a view of the front door. "I'm meeting Emily for dinner," she told him as he handed her a black-and-gold menu.

Antonio bowed and stepped back as the waiter joined him. "I will keep my eyes open for her and send her right back," he said formally and turned away.

Rebecca ordered a tonic with a twist of lime and "lots and lots of ice" and sat back to scan the menu. Half an hour later she was on her second tonic and decided to call Emily's cell phone. As she dialed the number, she leaned back in the padded seat, absentmindedly stirring her drink with a black plastic straw. The call went to Emily's mailbox and she began to get frustrated.

"My God, Em, what has gotten into you? Why aren't you answering your cell phone?" She waved the waiter away and picked up the menu again. Fifteen minutes later she slid out of her seat for a visit to the ladies room and ordered another tonic before leaving the booth.

Antonio was waiting for her when she got back. "Emily isn't coming after all?" he wondered and Rebecca began to get worried.

She glanced at her watch and picked up her cell phone again. "I'm sure I have the right night. Just let me give her another call." Emily's recorded voice came on again and Rebecca began angrily, "Where *are*…," then stopped and started again, "I'm at Antonio's waiting for you. Didn't you get my message? Are you OK? I'm getting worried. *Please call me!*" She hung up the phone, slapped it down next to her drink.

By eight o'clock, she realized that Emily was not coming at all and slouched in her booth, worried and disappointed. "I guess we got our wires crossed," she told the waiter, "but I'll go ahead and order." She chose a fresh sole francese and a small salad and sat nursing another tonic and lime as she waited. "Darn well not going to waste the babysitter," she grumbled and tucked into her dinner.

When Rebecca got home later that night, Bianca was curled up on the couch in front of the television and the children were all asleep upstairs. On the screen a loud group of people were trying to climb a pole before sliding down a muddy bank on garbage can covers.

"That looks inviting," Rebecca observed dryly and slung her bag over the back of a dining-room chair. She paid Bianca and sent her home, then hurried to the phone in the kitchen.

One more time, I'll give it one more try and then no more tonight. She listened to the phone ring through to the Emily's phone mailbox again and this time didn't bother to leave a message.

Emily, I'm really angry with you. Rebecca trudged upstairs and got ready for bed. And worried, she added. Tired as she was, Rebecca tossed and turned until, finally, at one-thirty in the morning she was able to drift off to sleep. Her dreams were chaotic and her night restless.

August second was hot and dry and each morning, as Emily came through the back door of 24 Officers' Row, she'd glance at the messy board with its one chalked message, August 15th... what? The tourists that came through History House were often hot and cranky.

"Why is this stove so old-fashioned?" "Why is the study so dusty?" and "Why in the world is the picture of Franklin Delano Roosevelt hanging on the wall? Shouldn't it be a framed copy of the U.S. Constitution?"

Emily wanted to ask them where they'd gone to school but took pity on the poor people trudging through the old house and answered the questions kindly. She knew how they felt. It was hot!

One afternoon she made a visit to Number 30 Officer's Row, the house the Audubon Society was using as their New Jersey southern headquarters. It was so hot she wanted to get out of the stuffy house and headed down the street, heat waves hovering over the asphalt. As she started up the front steps to Number 30 a door slammed and a tall, well-tanned woman came striding around the corner. Her short brown hair was shot through with gray and her eyes sparkled with amusement. She was dressed in a light blue shirt tucked into tan pants and tall riding boots and for a moment Emily wondered if she had hitched a horse to the back railing; then she thought, my heavens, she must be hot!

"Oy," the woman called, her voice hinting at a British background. "Hello, hello. I'm Jewel Carter, can I help you?" She stopped at the steps and added, "This is the Audubon Society." She grabbed Emily's hand, shaking it firmly.

Emily was fascinated and happy to meet her neighbor. "I'm curious about your house." She sat down on the step and stretched her legs out in front of her. "I'm also interested in one of your members, a young woman who often stands on the seawall in front of History House."

Jewel sat down next to her and laughed. "So you're the mysterious woman who takes care of Number 24…the museum… hmm. A young woman? No, no…nobody like that, just us old hens here, ha-ha-ha…By the bye, we aren't here all the time." She slapped at a mosquito and added, "Just once a month, here in the house. We spend most our time on Sandy Hook Bay…with the birds, of course."

Emily raised her eyebrows, smiled. It dawned on her the stranger on the seawall was not one of the "bird people," as John Rogers called them, and after a few more minutes of desultory conversation, she thanked Jewel and stood up, ready to make the walk back to History House. As she headed up Officers' Row, she thought about the stranger. The mystery had not been solved, but, as she slammed through the back door, she decided not to tell John Rogers. Why bother?

Back at Number 30, Jewel Carter watched through the dining-room window and turned to one of the volunteers who was busy sorting flyers on the big table. "An odd little duck, isn't she? Looks a little old-fashioned, aye? Maybe that's the way they make her dress. Tsk tsk!"

CHAPTER THIRTY-EIGHT

THE THUNDERSTORM

AUGUST 2009

O N A SULTRY August afternoon, a few days after her visit to the
Audubon Society, Emily was showing a group of delighted
senior citizens out the back door of History House. It was
the end of their tour and they were chattering about what they
had seen, their hands waving enthusiastically.

"Did you see the old icebox?" a white-haired octogenarian
laughed and they whispered excitedly among themselves. They'd
peered into the pantry and gushed over each and every one of
the items in the cupboard and on the counter. "Look at those
old cereal boxes and oh…look at the darling vase." Three ladies
dithered around the counter. "I just love the old tea set and silverware and, oh my, did you see the box of Aunt Jemima pancake
mix? What fun! And to think, we never thought of those as 'old-
fashioned,' did we?"

They'd moved like a swarm of harbor seals through the dining
room and into the living room, heads swerving back and forth as
they gazed around, and when the group looked into the officer's
study, they all but swooned. "Franklin Delano *Roosevelt*, oh, he was
so special. And of course he turned the country around lickety-
split. And his *wife*, Eleanor, now there was a *real* feminist! You
know, Hillary just loved her and even said that Eleanor 'spoke to
her.' What do you think of that?"

The ladies chattered among themselves, enchanted with their visit, and Emily had enjoyed the group. At least they have some appreciation of history, she thought. As she helped them down the back steps a loud rumble of thunder boomed across Fort Hancock followed by a flash of lightning that split the sky. The ladies screamed in excitement. "Hurry up, Folks," called the group leader. Then for added effect: "a *huge* storm is coming." She unfurled an umbrella and the group, giggling like a crowd of teenage girls, hustled to the bus as the rain started.

Emily closed the back door and hurried through the house, closing windows and drawing the drapes. As she came through the kitchen, the wind picked up and loud, fat drops of rain hit the windows. For just a minute, she heard the faint but distinct fragment of conversation somewhere in the house: *"storm outside… window…close the door…"*

Rats! Somebody's been left behind, she grumbled and turned back the way she'd come calling, "Hello, hello, somebody? Anybody?" But the house was empty. After a minute she shrugged her shoulders and returned to the kitchen muttering, "Imagination again!"

Emily stepped out onto the veranda to watch the storm as it moved in over the bay. The sound of the waves rode in on the wind and the sky boiled with angry, dark clouds. Sudden flashes of lightning outlined the trees along Officers' Row and the bay flung surf at the seawall. She shivered and dashed back inside and locked the door. Oh Lord, this certainly is *not* good driving weather. As though the idea had been in the back of her mind all along, Emily thought, I'll just camp out in one of the second-floor bedrooms. Yes, it wouldn't be the first time I've slept in my bra and panties, and she giggled as she raced up the stairs to the second floor.

The master bedroom had the biggest bed, the one the officer and his wife had shared, and she was relieved to find it was made up with sheets and a light blanket under the coverlet. Pulling the blanket back and plumping the pillows, she took off her watch and dropped it into the china bowl on the vanity and felt her way across the dark hallway to the bathroom. She washed her face in the bathroom sink, scrubbed her teeth with her index finger and looked at herself in the mirror. This feels like home, she told her reflection, and pulled a towel out of the linen closet.

Before returning to the master bedroom, she walked through the children's rooms. She patted the tan-and-orange plaid coverlet on the boy's bed and turned in a circle, gazing at the posters on the walls. She walked next door and, as she smoothed the pink spread, thought about the little girl in the photograph: the wide grin and tousled hair. In the baby's nursery, she picked up the Raggedy Ann doll and walked over to the window, looking out as the rain lashed the grounds. As she held the doll against her cheek, she was surprised to find her face wet with tears. Enough of this, she told herself sternly, dropped Raggedy Ann in the chair and walked back across the hall, scrubbing her face with her hands.

Emily dropped her khaki pants and light summer top over the back of the little bedroom chair by the window, crawled under the covers and turned off the bedside lamp. Lightning flashed over the bay and the wind rattled the windows, flinging rain in great gusts against the glass. She lay on her side and watched the storm outside, letting her mind wander: Did I remember to close the windows at home? Wait...my car windows? No, I remember closing them this morning...the windows downstairs? No, I closed all of them before coming upstairs. I wonder where that woman lives. Nearby? She's not with the Audubon Society... so where? Soon she drifted off into a restless sleep. That night, nobody stood on the seawall looking out over the bay.

The rain and wind stormed off the coast at dawn. When Emily woke up, the world outside the windows had a clean, fresh-scrubbed look, the sky a clear blue with a few fluffy clouds. The sun was already burning over the ocean and the water in the bay was as smooth as glass. She sat on the side of the bed, yawned, pushed her hair off her face and behind her ears. Yipes, she thought, peering sideways at a strand of lank hair. I think I need to visit the hair salon pretty soon. She pulled the strand in front of her face and looked at it with crossed eyes.

She lost interest and, stretching, tucked the strand of hair behind her ear as she rolled off the bed and wandered into the bathroom. A hot shower, *that's* what I need. She turned the water on in the shower and stepped under the stream, scrubbed her hair with the fat bar of soap from the soap dish and rubbed the lather over herself from head to foot, using her hands as a washcloth. After briskly rubbing herself with the towel, she wrapped the damp terrycloth around her body and peered into the linen closet. Okay, another towel to dry my wet hair? The only thing on the shelves was a pile of sheets, an old shower curtain, three boxes of lightbulbs and a small bottle of aspirin.

Somewhere in this house there's another towel, she thought and slipped downstairs to look under the kitchen sink. She unearthed a terrycloth dishtowel, wrapped it around her wet hair, and ran back upstairs. Sitting on the side of the bed, she hung her head down and toweled her hair briskly until it was dry, and carefully combed out the tangles until it fell softly around her face, dug around in her pocketbook to unearth her powder and lipstick and a wad of tissues and sat down at the vanity. She studied her reflection in the wavy old mirror and leaned back, bewildered. Her hair had grown so long it now fell in a smooth, almost silver pageboy. I absolutely have to get my hair cut: maybe next week or the week after…or maybe not at all. She turned her face one way and then the other. I rather like my new look, she thought as she gazed at herself. Hmm, and if I can find some scissors, how about some bangs for a change?

Emily pulled on her khaki pants and white shirt and quickly made the bed, pressed the coverlet over the blankets and pillows until there was no sign she'd slept there. She stood up and smoothed her pants down over her hips and, looking at her reflection again, thought: I want my sundresses. I want my towels and my toothbrush and toothpaste. I want my hairbrush and face creams and pajamas. She stopped herself, puzzled, and then finally put her feelings into words: I want to be *here!*

The rest of the day, Emily hid in her office, filling in her action report for John Rogers, trying to keep busy. Every now and then her cell phone chimed, but she ignored it and finally opened the desk drawer and tossed it inside. When tourists knocked at the back door, she invited them in, smiling vacantly, handed them brochures and told them to enjoy the house.

At noon she found half a sandwich in the icebox, filled a paper cup with coffee and carried them back to her desk, where she sat and absentmindedly ate her lunch. I think I've scared myself, she admitted as she took the coffee cup and waxed paper back to the kitchen. Then forgot the thought.

She cleaned up the kitchen, sat at her desk again and gazed at a pile of records that needed her attention but, instead, she picked up the photograph of the family. You look so familiar, she told the woman and then softly touched the soldier's face with her finger. She studied his lazy eyes and wide, smiling mouth and her heart beat faster. *Who are you?* She turned the picture one way and another, then stopped in amazement, jumped to her feet and headed for the hallway with the photo in her hand.

I know why this woman looks so familiar, she said excitedly. Stooping down in front of the group of framed photographs that hung on the wall next to the kitchen, she held the family photograph next to the one of the mother with her children. I *knew* it, I knew I'd seen you somewhere! She looked at the two old photographs side by side: one of an army officer and his family at the beach and the other, the radiant young mother, dark hair framing her pretty face, sitting on the front steps of the officer's house with her three children. Both were images of the same women and children, frozen in time. For a brief moment,

Emily felt a stab of sorrow. The officer's wife has a baby. She had another baby. She looked at the infant in her mother's lap and lost her train of thought. Then, smiling softly, Emily touched the man's face again, put the framed photo back on her desk and sat down in her office chair, gazing dreamily into the back hall. She realized that she was happy for the first time in months and it nearly moved her to tears.

As the afternoon sun started to sink in the west, Emily heard footsteps upstairs, somebody walking into the master bedroom, and then snatches of conversation.

"At home...here...safe..." A woman's soft voice floated down the stairs.

Emily turned her chair around and looked out the window at the open field. Three workmen were piling garden tools in the bed of a white pickup truck with *Sandy Hook Landscaping* printed on the truck door, a rare Sunday afternoon task. She watched them for a while, twirling a lock of hair around her little finger, thinking about her trip to the mainland. A man's soft laughter echoed in the hall by the kitchen and she heard the rush of someone darting past the office. Somehow she felt comforted and didn't bother to turn around.

The next day was Monday and the museum would be closed. No workmen or tourists around; the fort would be empty and she'd move to the officer's house. Upstairs, the footsteps and voice faded.

Emily walked out into the front hall and called softly up the staircase, "Tomorrow, I'll be coming back to live here. I don't want to anger you; I want to be with you. I won't be scared away." A breeze tossed one of the curtains in the kitchen, and upstairs a sigh drifted across the hallway and down the stairs.

The next afternoon, Emily moved into History House.

CHAPTER THIRTY-NINE

A MOVE TO FORT HANCOCK

AUGUST 2009

THAT EVENING, BEFORE she left for home, Emily stopped by the old garage where she'd found the bicycle, looked both ways to make sure no one was there and then dragged the door open, bracing it with a cement block before heading for home.

It was dinnertime by the time she pulled into her driveway in Atlantic Highlands. She turned on the kitchen light and tossed forgotten bills and catalogs on top of the stack of unopened mail, glanced into the refrigerator and went upstairs to pack.

Gnawing on a shriveled apple, she pulled her suitcase and an old canvas duffle out of the closet and piled them on the bed. As she walked back and forth between the bathroom and the bedroom, Emily recalled the day that Derek had packed to go to Afghanistan. It seemed so long ago she had almost forgotten how frightened she'd been. How things have changed, she thought, and then wondered just how much they *had* changed. She rubbed her eyes. What am I doing?

She pulled three sundresses and some pants off their hangers and piled them on the bed, wondered where Derek was and if he was all right; she packed her underwear, the dresses and some T-shirts and thought about what he would do if he couldn't reach her, felt regret, then rolled her toilet articles and makeup into a towel and thought about Rebecca. What would *she* say? Would she be worried? And Auntie Emily? She packed two towels and three washcloths and a bottle of Orchard Body Wash into the canvas bag and finally sat down on the bed.

"Okay, I *don't* know what I'm doing," she said out loud and started to cry. Somehow she knew she would never see Derek again, knew it was finally over. The bedroom window was open and an evening breeze ruffled the curtains. She looked out at the backyard and was shocked to see it was overgrown with green foliage, the flowerbeds smothered by weeds, the sheet hanging limply on the clothesline she had so carefully set up the month before. Exhausted, she lay down next to the suitcase and closed her eyes. As night fell, Emily slept alone on her side of the bed. She didn't dream and she didn't wake until the alarm went off the next morning and she didn't think about Derek again.

At ten thirty Emily left her home in Atlantic Highlands. She shoved her belongs into the Honda and headed back to History House. The day was going to be another scorcher. She turned her car toward Fort Hancock and when she crossed the causeway to Sandy Hook the water in the bay was still, no breeze tossing up little wavelets.

Sandy Hook was filling up with more vacation traffic and all the way up Hartshorne Drive she had to inch along behind cars filled with beach-goers hauling their beach umbrellas, chairs, toys, not to mention their sunburned children: everyone anxious to get to the ocean. By the time she reached the gate to Fort Hancock, she was sweating nervously and chewing on her thumbnail.

Emily arrived at the officer's house by noon and, relieved, pulled the Honda into the ruined garage. The dust had settled back onto the floor and the air was stuffy with the summer heat. The car will be safe here, she thought; nobody will ever find it.

She carried her suitcase and the big canvas bag into the officer's house and hurried back for the rest, pushed the garage door back into place and leaned the cement block against it, closing the Honda away from sight.

Emily stacked everything on the big bed in the master bedroom and thought, I feel at home already. The shampoo, toothbrush, toothpaste and towels went into the bathroom, stored in the linen closet. She hung her three sundresses in the walk-in closet off the master bedroom and her brush, face creams and makeup went on the glass-topped vanity. Looking around the bedroom, she spotted the woman's dresser by the wall and decided to put the rest of her clothes in one of the drawers. Piling her underwear, tops and khaki pants on top of the dresser, she pulled open the bottom drawer.

As it inched out, she saw that it was already in use, filled with heavy, dark drapes. What in the world? Emily wondered and felt the fabric between her fingers. These are the yuckiest drapes I've ever seen. Why would *anyone* want to hang these ugly-looking things in such a nice house? She closed the drawer and opened the next one, only to discover the next two were filled with more of the dusty old drapes. Ugh, she said in disgust and picked up her clothing and carried it over to the officer's dresser, carefully folding her things and packing them away in its empty drawers.

CHAPTER FORTY

AIR RAIDS AND BEACON LIGHTS

1943-1945

B ETTY STOOD IN the middle of the living room and glared at the blackout curtains. Why can't James help me take these ugly things down, she wondered crossly. After all, the Führer is dead and the war in Europe is over. Japan is on the other side of the world and now we don't even see Sergeant Jonah so much anymore. She wrinkled her nose and her stomach rumbled. They hold dirt too, she complained, and it's making me sick.

Over the war years when the air-raid siren started to wail Betty would hurry around the house pulling the heavy blackout curtains across the windows. Ugly things, she'd think as she hauled their weight over the darkness. If this damnable war ever ends, I'll pull these down and pack them away so I never have to look at them again.

James would leave his study and help turn off all the lights, leaving a dim lamp in the living room behind the wing chair. Together they'd huddle around the family radio in the living room and laugh with Charlie McCarthy or Amos and Andy as they listened for the sound of enemy planes in the distance.

There was a space where the living-room curtains didn't completely close and Betty could see a sliver of the beacon lights from the small airfield on the mainland. She felt secure, knowing that someone was out there scanning the sky. Sometimes Sergeant Jonah, the Fort Hancock air-raid warden, would stop by and chat with James, and Betty could hear their low voices and soft laughter in the back hall; see the dim beam of the warden's flashlight through the space, bouncing over the grass as he headed across the side yard to Della's house checking that no lights were left on or blackout curtains open to allow enemy planes a target if they roared overhead.

The air raids scared her but they brought her family together, and in an odd way she had welcomed the sound of the siren as it rose and fell in the night. When the all clear sounded its hoarse honk across Fort Hancock, the children would help Betty open the curtains, and these evenings James would put his arm around her and smile into her eyes as he led upstairs. Later they would fall asleep in each other's arms; but now, even with the war in Europe over, he still closed himself in his study anxious to hear the news from the Pacific. "This war is almost over," he told Betty, "I'm sure I can see the end at last." Then his study door would close and she would go upstairs, read to the children and tuck them in. Night after night she'd turn off their lights and sit at her sewing machine, making sheets and pillowcases for the "boys in the Pacific." It seemed to her that she was always waiting for her husband. With her feet pushing the pedal up and down and her fingers feeding the fabric under the needle, she realized she was becoming a very lonely woman.

All through the spring of 1945 Betty wandered over to the seawall when the children were finally asleep and James was still in his study. From the top of the wall she could see the bay and the mainland in the distance. The two beacon lights continued to sweep across the sky, crisscrossing each other as they guarded against the Japanese submarines and planes that the wives whispered about in the Officers' Club now.

Betty wondered about these rumors: would the Japanese come all the way to New Jersey…*could* they? She doubted that, but didn't want to ask James and was nervous about it, anyway. "What if they did," she asked herself out loud, "and I wasn't watching for them? What then? Oh dear, I could never forgive myself." The thought made her even more frightened and alone. She'd stand there watching fascinated as they lit up the night, twisting her wedding ring around her finger, her dark hair tangled by the evening breeze. Someday, she'd tell herself, someday there will be no more beacon lights, no more blackouts, no more rations, no more enemies. All of this will be over and we'll be safe, again. Someday, the war will be over!

Late at night, James would come up and sit down on the bed, then lean over and kiss her lips, stroke his hand down over her shoulder and hip and whisper, "Baby, baby, I love you." Only once did she roll over and into his arms, but most nights she never woke up and never knew.

CHAPTER FORTY-ONE

A LIGHT IN THE WINDOW

AUGUST 2009

THE WEEK AFTER Emily moved to History House the weather turned hot and dry, again, as if the storm had drained every drop of moisture from the air and carried it along as it rumbled off to sea. Everyday the sun would rise out of the ocean and travel a cloudless sky until setting over the bay in the evening.

Each morning Emily spooned coffee into the coffee pot and while it perked, she trudged down the back steps to peer through the garage window to make sure Derek's car was still safe inside. "Who'd take it?" she chided herself, but the next morning she'd head out the back to the garage, again. By the end of the week, thick gray dust covered the Honda like a shroud and she knew she wouldn't bother to look anymore.

The third morning after her move she stood in the middle of the kitchen floor, gazing into the almost empty can of Maxwell House coffee and it dawned on her that she'd not given a single thought to stocking the pantry or refrigerator before her move, had not a crumb of bread left and only a few scoops of coffee. She scraped the last grains into the pot and, later, sat down to make a list, doodling cats' faces on the pad of paper and twirling a blond curl around her finger. The rest of the morning she spent polishing the furniture, dabbing English Polish on a cloth and rubbing the wood until it shone. The afternoon was filled with tourists, cameras slung around their necks, anxious to see how people lived in the 1940s, ohing and ahhing at what they saw. At the end of the day the grocery list sat on her desk, blank but for the cats' faces. Oh well, she thought and left the list on the desk.

At twilight Emily backed the car out of the garage and headed down Hartshorne Drive and over to the mainland just as the streetlights came on. A few miles from the Highlands Bridge was a small Foodmart and she turned into the parking lot and pulled up in a dark corner near four large, green Dumpsters. The idea of running into someone she knew made her anxious, now, almost afraid. What if they ask how I am? Emily wondered. What would I say: I'm living in a deserted army base in a museum? My God, they'd think I lost my mind, and if they asked about Derek? Good Lord, what a thought! She felt guilty and sad, but headed inside, collected some money from the ATM machine and grabbed a basket. Rolling down the unfamiliar aisles, she filled the basket with cans of vegetables and baked beans, fruit in light syrup and spaghetti with tomato sauce, a gallon of milk, three family-sized boxes of cold cereal, two wedges of cheddar cheese, two cans of Maxwell House coffee, a box of tea bags and a large tub of butter. She added four loaves of bread, three containers of peanut butter and, on a whim, seven large bars of organic dark chocolate.

The cashier was a bored young woman with a ponytail and a dusting of freckles across her cheeks. She was chewing gum busily and as she ran Emily's items across the scanner she glanced up. "You gonna go out'n live at the end of the world or somethin', you know, with all this stuff? She snapped her gum rudely and Emily smiled thinly, shrugged.

"I'm expecting company and I just moved in."

"The chocolate looks good, anyway." The cashier snapped her gum again, rolled it into one side of her mouth and added, "I love chocolate." Emily smiled again and stacked the grocery bags back in the basket and headed to the car. What does she *want*, some of my chocolate? Add it to her gum for heaven's sake?

By the time she pulled up behind History House, it was dark and a sliver of a moon hung overhead. Emily emptied the car and lined the bags up on the back porch before driving the Honda into the garage again. She emptied bag after bag of cans and loaves, boxes and containers until the tops of the counters and the kitchen table were filled, stood back and decided she rather liked what she'd bought: easy things to cook, nothing to bake in the oven, things she could even eat out of the container, sandwiches and fruit, cereal in a bowl with milk, coffee, tea. And chocolate! Nodding happily, she started to put everything away.

Done with the groceries, Emily crossed the veranda and turned down Officers' Row, a warm evening breeze tossing her hair around her face. She'd started taking a nightly walk when twilight turned Fort Hancock into a deserted little island. The water in the bay reflected the lights on the mainland and the leaves rustled overhead. Every morning she'd straightened out the bedroom and kitchen, hiding any sign of her living there. But at night, when the last tourist disappeared down Hartshorne Drive, she'd close the back door and lock it, straighten out her little office and close the door behind her. She'd walk through the rooms and shut off the lights, leaving on the ones in the kitchen and hall, eat a light supper and then slip out the front door, breathing in the warm air and flexing her shoulders, relaxing now that the house was hers again.

At the end of the street Emily stood looking out at the bay and then turned back. Her first week! She smiled slightly and shook her head. Who'd ever imagine this…Derek? She frowned, swallowed a sudden lump in her throat and then thought: Becca, Ruthie, Jena? Robin Drury? Oh my God! She laughed out loud and headed back down Officers' Row. As she passed the house next to History House she stopped short, straining her eyes in the dark. Large maple trees lined the street and the top floor of 24 Officers' Row was just visible through a thick web of leaves. Emily's heart beat faster. Was that a dim light shining from the window of the master bedroom? Did I forget to turn off the lights? No, she shook her head. I always turn off all the lights except the kitchen and hall…all the lights. I wouldn't *dare* leave the bedroom light on. A shadow passed across the window and she froze for just a second, then scolded her active imagination: Just the leaves as they move in the breeze, Em, don't be silly!

She hurried across the veranda and through the front door, leaving it a jar. In case I have to escape, she whispered. Please God, don't let someone be here, someone waiting for me upstairs in the bedroom. She stood still and craned her neck, listening for the creak of footsteps overhead or some other unusual sound. Nothing moved but the leaves outside. A branch tapped against one of the living room windows and she jumped. Okay, she scolded herself, enough! I have to take care of this one way or another, and arming herself with a kitchen knife she crept up the stairs, stopping at each step to listen, peering into the upstairs hall. The branch tapped at the window again and the floors creaked and complained, but upstairs it was dark, quiet, and no light shone from the master bedroom. No voices, no steps and no lights after all and Emily headed back to the kitchen, scolding her imagination again and sending a little 'thank you' heavenward.

After putting away the kitchen knife and pouring herself a glass of milk, she sat and relaxed for a few minutes before heading upstairs to bed, happy that all was calm and quiet; but as she turned into the upstairs hall, a soft sign drifted down the stairs and faded away.

That night she had a dream: she was in a long corridor; a small table sat under a window at the far end and yellow light spilled from a single lamp. Rooms led off left and right and she was hurrying, anxious, looking into each room. A man appeared in the hall in front of her…Derek! She tried but she couldn't catch up with him and he didn't seem to hear her calling his name.

Frustrated, she followed him into one of the rooms, a room that she seemed to know. Was it the master bedroom in History House? He finally turned around, but it was a stranger: tall, blond, oddly familiar. He smiled and she felt as if she were fainting, falling into the dark. The next morning only fragments of the dream remained, leaving Emily bemused and slightly troubled.

As the days went by, her mind returned to the dream over and over again and she wondered why the stranger looked so familiar. Who is this man, she asked herself on more than one occasion, and why does he trouble me so much?

CHAPTER FORTY-TWO

A KISS BEFORE DAWN

AUGUST 2009

THE HOT WEATHER continued and cicadas sang their loud, raucous songs throughout the long afternoons. Emily began to spend the evenings out on the seawall. She'd often thought about the strange young woman, had wondered why she found her way there so often. Now, as she stood looking out at the mainland, she understood how this stranger must feel.

Where the expanse of water met the mainland shore, the lights would come on one after the other and the sound of distant traffic would lull her anxious thoughts. When the last of the daylight left the western sky, she'd go back inside and lock the door, pull the drapes across the windows to shut out the dark and walk through the downstairs rooms, running her fingers lightly across the tables and along the chair backs. Time seemed to stand still. I'm never going to leave, she told herself. This is my house now.

One night she stopped outside the officer's study and gazed through the door, stooped down and crawled under the velvet rope. She touched the desk with her fingertips and sat in the office's chair. Looking around the small room, she tapped a few of the keys on the typewriter, then glanced at the open newspaper. This was the first time she'd been inside the study, had always only looked through the door. The feeling of nostalgia suddenly overwhelmed her and she squeezed her eyes shut for a minute.

The old Philco, with its cracked glass dial and wooden knobs, stood next to the desk. Emily leaned forward and idly turned one of the knobs. At first there was empty silence; then the dial lit up and a low hissing sound issued from the speaker. After a few minutes, a low voice broke into the static: *"The complexities of the war in the European Theater…"* More static drowned out the voice for a minute; then another voice announced: *"Gabriel Heatter…"* More static: *"…there's good news tonight"* And then that voice, too, was lost. As suddenly as it had come, the static faded away and the dial turned dark.

Emily frowned and stood up: The war in the "European Theater? She crawled back under the velvet rope. Why are they talking about that old stuff? How about the war in the mountains of Afghanistan? And what in the world is a Gabriel Heater? Some kind of good news, environmentally-friendly home heating system? She dusted herself off and headed off to bed.

Mornings, when Emily awoke in the officer's bed, she'd roll over until she was facing the windows and gaze out at the bay before padding into the bathroom for her morning shower. The old bed was surprisingly comfortable and she felt as if she were safe in some big, warm cocoon. Safe and warm, she told herself. Safe and warm in this house where I belong.

One morning as she lay dozing, the faint sound of pots and pans rattling around downstairs crept into her dreams, then the sound of the oven door closing and a pan moving across the stovetop. Emily curled up on her side, and a smile touched her lips. After a few minutes, she heard a wisp of the odd conversations that had been drifting in and out of her consciousness: *"Children…yes… milk…oleomargarine on the toast…"*

Then it faded away along with the morning kitchen sounds. Emily turned over and buried her face in her pillow and by the time she crawled out of bed and headed for the shower, the big house was empty and still. By noon she had forgotten about it.

The following night she felt the first soft kiss. Just before dawn, when the wind was still and the water in the bay lay quiet, she felt a presence by the bed, and then lips against her own. Blinking in the dark, still half asleep but strangely unafraid she pressed her fingers over her mouth and sighed softly before falling back into some interrupted dream.

Now her nights were filled with extraordinary visions and the knowledge that someone was near, leaning over her, his lips against hers. Sometimes she felt his hand on her shoulder, stroking her arm and down over her hips, brushing the hair away from her face. She was never alarmed, never woke shaking in fear. He came more often, touching her, holding her and whispering: "Baby, baby, I love you"; then vanishing into the dark, leaving her limp and exhausted. I think I'm lost, she told herself. I think I'm lost now but it's okay.

Twenty-four Officers' Way was becoming filled with a strange energy and she rarely felt alone.

When tourists arrived, Emily greeted them like guests and graciously showed them around. She was the hostess, put away the guestbook and, when the brochures were gone, didn't bother to put them out again. She started to hold the picture of the officer and his family in her hands; pressing it against her lips, touching the soldier's face over and over again. She took the picture out of its frame, folded it over, hiding his wife and children, and gazed at the soldier: Who are you? Who *are* you? Why do I want you so?

Late one afternoon John Rogers came out to the house and when Emily came to the screen door he frowned, thought her appearance and behavior were decidedly odd, although he couldn't put his finger on what it was. It *had* been awhile, he told himself, what with his vacation with June and Julie. But who would begrudge him his two weeks camping in the Desert of Maine and then, with all the work that was waiting for him when he got back to his office…Well, what could he say? Anyway, decidedly odd, he thought.

"Emily, you okay?" he asked when she opened the screen door.

"Hi John," Emily stepped back, "let's sit in the kitchen. I have some fresh perked coffee on the stove. So much more comfortable than that little old office, don't you think?" She led the way to the kitchen. John slid into the seat behind the high chair and had to admit she looked radiant: dressed in a red-and-white sundress, her silvery blond hair in a smooth pageboy, soft bangs falling over her forehead.

"Do you need any supplies? Anything I can get for you? Is everything okay out here?" He watched, fascinated, as she arranged two cups on a small tray and added milk to a white, cow-shaped cream pitcher, poured coffee and carried the tray to the table, taking the chair across from him.

" I don't need anything, John." She touched a finger to her cheek, thought for a minute and then opened her eyes wide, "Gosh, I forgot to finish my reports. It's pretty busy out here now and I have to make sure everyone is taken care of, you know. It's so important with the war and all. I will get them done, though, I promise."

"Uh, Emily, you're sure your okay?" John frowned, added milk to his coffee and thought: "War?" He wondered about Derek but didn't want to ask, figured that was something she would certainly tell him and of course things really were heating up in Afghanistan.

Emily blushed and gazed out the window for a few minutes, smiling dreamily. "I'm just swell," she assured him and tipped her cup to her lips. "Just swell. Everything is fine here. I don't need anything, honest. "

John was feeling decidedly uneasy, but he finished his coffee and pushed the cup away. "Do we have anymore business before we call it a day, Em?" This is awkward, he thought.

"No, and it's getting late." Emily glanced at her wristwatch, "maybe we better finish our visit some other time." She slid out of her chair and smoothed her dress over her hips, waited for John and patted his arm as she walked him to the back door

John Rogers shook his head as he headed to his truck and muttered, "I think she's taking this museum thing a little too... ah...seriously. I'll just have to check in more often now." Then he drove away without giving it another thought, and it was only later that he recalled that day and wondered if he should have done something right then and there. But what? he asked himself.

CHAPTER FORTY-THREE

REBECCA AND JENA

AUGUST 15, 2009

Jena Rose headed out for her lunch hour. She was looking forward to an iced tea and one of Adalet's "Jersey Fresh" salads. Finally, after digging around in her backpack, she was plugged into her MP3 player listening to the Black Eyed Peas' "I Gotta Feeling."

Emily had always been amused by Jena Rose. Petite and ladylike, with a face and figure like a Barbie doll, Jena invariably caused men to turn into nurturing, macho he-men, which she viewed with disgust. Three years earlier, she had single-handedly packed all her belongs, including a small table, two chairs, a store mannequin, three boxes of books, an old, blue bubble-backed Apple computer and keyboard, a carton of Spam, three large bags of dog food and a futon onto a small trailer attached to her aging black Taurus, and, along with a small white dog named Hank moved lock, stock, and barrel from California to New Jersey. She'd once confided in Emily that she had chosen New Jersey because she was enamored of Tony Soprano.

Jena paused to look at an especially delicious pair of black Perez Lopez open-toed pumps with four-inch heels. A touch on her arm made her heart leap into her throat.

"I called to you from across the street," Rebecca Wade said apologetically as Jena spun around.

"My God, Becca, you scared me to death. I almost jumped out of my skin!" Jena gasped and pulled her MP3 ear buds out of her ears, then managed a smile. "I'm sorry, I didn't hear you. I'm on my lunch hour and going to Adalet's for a salad...wanna come?"

Rebecca looked longingly down the street toward the tearoom but shook her head. "Actually, I'm on my way to a doctor's appointment, but I saw you and, well...I wanted to know if you'd heard from Emily." She looked at Jena, a small frown on her face. "I've called her over and over and keep leaving messages on her answering machine and cell phone." She paused for a minute. "In fact, our little girlfriend stood me up last Friday. We were planning to go out for dinner, and guess what? No show! I'm really beginning to get worried."

Jena gazed at Rebecca and shook her head. "I don't know, Becca," she said, then added, "In fact, I called her a couple of weeks ago and asked her why she hadn't been coming to yoga. She sounded like she missed us and would come the next Monday and then didn't show up." Jena thought for a minute. "Look, I'm finishing up barber school this week and then I'll be heading to California to see my folks. I should be back by September first. Why don't we get together and drive out to Fort Hancock and see this famous house, find out what's going on with Emily?"

Rebecca quickly agreed and the two women decided to confirm the trip by phone when Jena returned to New Jersey. Another few more minutes of idle chatter and an air kiss and Rebecca turned back to her car. Jena headed to Adalet's for her lunch.

Neither woman could possibly know that they'd be too late.

CHAPTER FORTY-FOUR

MAUDE PEPPER AND EMILY

AUGUST 15, 2009

EMILY CAME DOWNSTAIRS and dropped her bag on the desk. She glanced at the blackboard outside the kitchen with its chalked date and wondered if she could find out what it was, who had left it. Maybe later, she told herself and then added, or maybe not at all. She smoothed her hair, fluffed her bangs and thought: The blackboard bothers me. I don't think it belongs here. She quickly pushed the thought out of her mind.

She wandered restlessly into the kitchen and filled the percolator with water, spooned coffee into the basket, then looked out the window. It was going to be another hot, sunny day, "a scorcher," as Auntie Emily would say. Emily wore her red-and-white sundress and had brushed her hair until it shone. She'd glanced at herself in the mirror and touched up her lips with the red CVS lipstick. Standing back, she'd admired the look: red-and-white dress, red lipstick and soft pageboy. "Nice," she'd told the mirror.

Maude Pepper had wanted to visit the History House Museum ever since she had read an article about it in the *Jersey Journal*. Now that she had lost Joe, God rest his soul, she found time on her hands, so on this hot, sunny August day she decided to visit Fort Hancock.

Maude had been in high school during World War II and she remembered it very well: the air-raid sirens and blackout curtains, the War Bonds that cost a dime in school, the wooden roller skates...steel was for the war effort, not toys...and, of course, the ration stamps that her mother used whenever she went food shopping. Maude Pepper smiled as she remembered standing with her girlfriends by the side of the road, waving small American flags and blowing kisses at the long lines of army trucks as the convoys went by day after day. Maude would blush with delight when the boys hung out the back of the trucks and shouted at the young girls, "We love you! Wait for us, Blondie! Hubba, hubba, ya got swell shapes, gals!"

Then in 1944, when Maude started her last year in high school, Joe had joined the navy. "To go get the enemy once and for all," he told her and gave her a ring with a tiny diamond that had belonged to Grandma Pepper. "I want you to wait for me," he said, his voice sounding grown-up and serious, and Maude had been scared but delighted.

She spent the next year lighting a candle in St. Anthony's Roman Catholic Church every afternoon on her way home from school and attending mass every Sunday morning, praying for Joe's safe return. When Joe came home they had, indeed, married at St. Anthony's.

Of course, she had to admit with some embarrassment, since then she hadn't kept up the trips to St. Anthony's, but she and Joe had had a good marriage and she missed him. So it was with some nostalgia that Maude Pepper turned her car south on the Garden State Parkway.

Maude parked behind a row of big, yellow brick homes and looked out her car window at Fort Hancock. This was the first time she'd ever been on an army base. Of course, Joe, God rest his soul, had been on a navy destroyer and had been sent to the South Pacific, so she never had reason to go to an army base. Once he'd come home, her husband had immediately gone to work for the U.S. Post Office and neither of them had ever looked back.

This was an interesting experience; the big, wide army base with its row upon row of yellow barracks and old brick buildings, standing along a dusty road, tall pine trees towering overhead. She looked back at the officers' houses, stoically facing the bay, then opened her car door and started walking to the one with the sign *History House* hanging by the back door. Just down the road was a huge field. Did they play ballgames there? Maude wondered as she climbed the back steps. This field is big enough for a football game or two.

"Hello, hello," she called and knocked on the screen door. A minute later a pretty young woman appeared at the door and opened it. She was dressed in a red-and-white cotton sundress, white wedge-heeled sandals, and her blond hair fell in a soft pageboy. Wow, Maude thought, she actually looks like she belongs here, very nineteen forties...sort of like Mother. Well, Mother back in her thirties, that is. Maude smiled and introduced herself and the young woman smiled back.

"I'm Emily," she said," Please come in. I'll show you around."

She stood back and Maude joined her in the hall. To their right was a wonderfully bright and tidy kitchen that immediately reminded Maude of her childhood. Crisp white curtains covered the windows and the black-and-white enamel table was set for a family, three places and a white highchair with a pink-and-white lamb stenciled on the back. Coffee perked briskly in the little percolator on the stove. Emily stood back as Maude admired the bright wallpaper, a small smile on her lips.

"Oh, this reminds me of Mother's house," Maude said wistfully. "We had paper like that: cherries and ivy leaves. It was such a happy room, even during that cursed war." She peeked into the pantry and patted her hair. "My husband Joe, God rest his soul, spent many, many days with me in Mother's kitchen." She smiled demurely.

Maude admired the dining room and living room as Emily excused herself to turn the flame down under the coffee. She rejoined Maude outside the officer's study, watching her reaction carefully. Maude paused, puzzled. "Just look at those relics," she exclaimed. "An old Royal typewriter, and oh, my...just look at President Roosevelt, he was *such* a good man. We loved him," she said softly, and continued, "these are *real* antiques. Oh, my, does that mean *I'm* an antique? Ha-ha...Hmm... This room does seem to make one feel, ah...strange, though. Like someone is still sitting there! Don't you think so?" Emily smiled but didn't answer and headed for the front hall.

Maude was happy to follow Emily up the stairs to the bedrooms. She crooned over the children's rooms and nursery. "My children are all grown up and gone. I have two girls and a boy and five adorable grandchildren." She stroked the blanket on the crib. "My oldest grandchild is getting married soon and that means I will be a *great*-grandmother, ha-ha...oh, mercy me." She looked out of the nursery window. "Is that a football field down there?"

Emily stood next to her and looked out. "No, it's a parade ground where the army assembles, uh...*assembled* when Fort Hancock was active, of course." She laughed and smoothed her hair, then led her guest into the hall, "and here is the sewing room," she said as they looked through the door.

Maude laughed aloud. "My word, can you imagine sitting in here and pumping away at that old Singer? And just look at the dress form. Kind of uh...shapely, wasn't she?"

Emily was amused. "So *that* is what that mannequin thing is called," she said. "I've been wondering but was embarrassed to ask."

"Oh, my dear," Maude gazed at the dress form. "All women had a good dress form back then. They'd fit their dresses to them, pin them up and then sew the fabric on the machine. I used to call my mother's Mrs. Spindle. Hmmm, don't know where I got that from."

The two women smiled at each other as they walked across the hall, but at the top of the stairs, Maude stopped short. "Did you hear *that*? A woman's voice? I'm sure. Maybe someone has come in, but it *did* sound like she was right here…upstairs with us."

Emily didn't respond but shook her head and calmly ushered her guest down the stairs. "Sometimes the house groans and creaks because it's so old." She invited Maude for a coffee in the kitchen. "Of course, there *are* stories and strange rumors. I'll tell you when we sit down. She brought the coffeepot to the table and plopped a hot pad down. As she filled two of the white coffee mugs, she told Maude about the old officer's house and its mysterious history.

"Not that anyone believes it," she finished, putting a mug in front of her guest. "But I have to say, I've heard things here, too. John Rogers, he's the park ranger here, says it's just the old walls 'talking to each other.' I don't even pay any attention anymore." The two women sat over their coffee and chatted until the sun moved toward the bay and shadows began to gather.

When Maude left History House, she thanked Emily warmly for a good tour and climbed back into her car. As she turned the key in the ignition, she leaned down and took a last look at the old house. "Sweet girl," she said out loud. "Very interesting way of dressing, hmm, I wonder if it's her uniform or something." She looked carefully in both directions, then pulled onto the main road. "Still," she added, "there's something very odd about this museum. Something very odd, indeed."

And then she shivered.

CHAPTER FORTY-FIVE

SANDY HOOK
AUGUST 15

EMILY
AUGUST 15, 2009: LATE AFTERNOON

As the afternoon breeze swept through the house, Emily poured the last of the coffee into a paper cup and slipped out onto the veranda to watch the sun set over the water. The seagrass was brown now, dry from the August sun, the water in the bay apathetic, smooth as gray glass, small waves just beginning to ripple with the dusk. The sound of the cicadas was fading to a low, lazy hum. As Emily stood there, her mind began to drift and she felt a slight chill, even in the evening heat. They say your life flashes through your mind when you're drowning, she thought. Am I drowning? She hugged herself. I miss you, Derek. Where are you? Are you safe? Are you still alive?

Since his unit had moved into the Afghani mountains she had felt lost, but realized with a start that in the past two weeks she had not given much thought to their life together. She ran her fingers lightly across the railing as her thoughts wandered back to their little house on the mainland. She sighed and acknowledged that until now, she hadn't given a thought to Derek. She looked around and frowned. What am I doing? What am I doing?

She hadn't been home since moving her belongings out to Fort Hancock two weeks before, had almost forgotten her cute Cape-style home with its trim lawns and flowering shrubs, things she had taken such pride in. She looked back through the big front door, and immediately her anxious thoughts seemed to still. She smiled, thought about the kisses, the gentle touches that woke her in the night, the beloved face in the photograph. Her heart beat faster and she caught her breath.

She moved to the front of the veranda and smoothed her sundress over her hips. As the sun sank in the west and shadows were thrown across the lawn, the strange young woman came around the side of the house and climbed up on the seawall. Again, she was dressed in the red-and-white cotton sundress, her dark hair ruffled by the breeze. As usual she gazed out over the water, her face remote and still. As Emily watched, the stranger began to twist the ring on her finger and suddenly Emily could hear the young woman's thoughts. Faintly, at first, and then as if the words were in her own head, she heard a soft, familiar voice.

"All these years people just like my family and I have lived in fear and terror and now...now it has ended...ended with a suicide and a poison cloud of death and destruction." The young woman dabbed at her eyes with a tissue.

"I've always thought of these far-off people as the "enemy," a threat to my happiness, but now, as I stand here safe by the seawall and think about all I've heard today, I suddenly realize they are just...people." She wiped her eyes again.

"Here I am next to my home, safe with my husband coming home soon with the children, the war has ended and I feel what? I feel... guilt! I'm alive...alive, and so many other mothers are not. So many children, gone. It's all so wrong!" She tucked the tissue into a pocket in her sundress. *"Oh, what a terrible secret. I'll have to live with this all my life."*

The words faded away with a sigh, and suddenly Emily's longing and confusion disappeared and she was filled with a nameless ecstasy, a focus. She put her empty cup on the railing and, as she stepped off the porch and crossed the dry grass to join the stranger, the woman turned, her dark hair framing her face, bangs falling softly over her forehead. She smiled and then Emily knew why she looked so familiar. Of course, she whispered, the photos: the photo in my office, the photo by the kitchen…the officer's wife! She quickened her step, brushed back her hair and never thought: how very odd!

BETTY
AUGUST 15, 1945: LATE AFTERNOON

Betty stood on the seawall, twisting her wedding ring on her finger and thinking about what she had heard that day. The strange and awful atomic bombs, dropped on Japan the week before, had ended the war. James wouldn't be sent away, but thousands upon thousands were dead: men, women, and children. She thought about the stories coming out of Europe now, stories of terrible camps where people were imprisoned, where millions had died, people like Anna's doctor and his family. She thought about mothers and fathers and babies who had suffered because of the overwhelming evil. Then she thought about the American President's death, how for days she had stood outside the study door, gazing at the portrait of President Roosevelt and weeping in sorrow.

"All these years," she said softly, "people just like my family and I have lived in fear and terror and now…now it has ended… ended with a suicide and a poison cloud of death and destruction and now even our President is gone."

Betty felt guilt and a terrible sorrow and it occurred to her that she'd been carrying this burden for a long time, had been feeling slightly sick to her stomach lately with the stress of the past few months of war in the Pacific.

I've always thought of these far-off people as the enemy, a threat to my happiness, but now, as I stand here safe by the seawall and think about all I've heard today, I suddenly realize they are just…people.

She looked at the smooth water in the bay. The wind swept past her and tossed her hair. Here I am next to my home, safe with my husband coming soon with the children, the war has ended and I feel what? I feel…guilt! Betty turned to look back at the house: her house, her home, and the home she shared with her husband and children. "I'm alive," she said out loud, "alive, and so many other mothers are not. So many children, gone." She sighed. "It's all so wrong!" She knew she could never tell her husband or her parents, or even Joyce. Tell them what she was feeling now. Oh, what a terrible secret. I'll have to live with this all my life.

As she started to turn away she saw a sudden movement and glanced back. A young woman had appeared on the veranda and stood watching her. Betty squinted in the reflection off the water. The woman was about her age and had long hair, so light blond it shone silver in the afternoon sun. The stranger smiled and started down the steps, pausing to put a paper cup on the railing, and as she came across the grass Betty smiled back, puzzled, and then gave a small wave. She knows me and she looks familiar. Who is she? And why was she on my veranda?

The young woman looked at her with a terrible longing in her blue eyes. "No, you don't know me but you're everything I want to be," she said softly. "You have everything I always wanted. I know what you're thinking; I hear what you're thinking. You don't need to feel so sad. You have a long and happy life ahead: children, and another baby soon, and," she sighed, "your husband…here with you, alive and well." She pressed her hands across her belly. "Listen to me, the time will come when these terrible things will be just another chapter in the history books and what you feel now? It will not be just your guilty secret. I know this." She lowered her voice. "I can help you. Yes, I know I can help you. Don't worry, everything will be okay, really."

Betty reached out to the stranger and as she touched the young woman's hand, she felt the burden of guilt and sorrow lift. At the same time relief and joy filled her heart. Finally, someone who was telling her everything would be all right. How did she know? How *could* she know? And a new baby? She placed one hand lightly on her stomach and thought about the night James had come to bed early; how she wakened and had responded, held her arms up as he leaned over her and how she'd felt happy and safe for a little while. A sudden breeze kicked up waves in the bay and then grew stronger, shaking the leaves along Officers' Row. For a few moments the sun seemed to dim, the sky darkened and the cicadas stopped their monotonous strumming. The two women stood looking at each other for a few moments, then smiled and moved together until, if one were looking, they'd think that only one young woman was standing on the seawall. The breeze grew still and the sun brightened. In the bay the water shimmered, then was smooth as glass again. One cicada started singing and then was joined by the rest.

Inside History House the chalk date on the little blackboard, August 15th, slowly faded away.

As evening fell, Betty blotted her cherry red lipstick with a toilet tissue. She sat back on the vanity seat and looked at herself. Long hair, so light blond it shone silver in the setting sun, framed her heart-shaped face and short bangs fell softy across her forehead. Large blue eyes fringed with thick Elizabeth Taylor lashes looked back at her. Downstairs the screen door opened and she heard James' voice calling the children as he came through the kitchen, heard him laugh as the door slammed behind him. As their voices moved through the dim house, she smoothed her hair again, stood up and turned to go downstairs. A slow smile suddenly appeared and she laughed softly, rested her hand on her rounded belly, felt the breath catch in her throat. James, the children and a new baby. She shivered and wrapped her arms around herself and, momentarily, felt a faint sorrow for something she knew she'd lost, but wasn't quite sure what it was. Then she smiled again. "The war is over," she said to herself. "Yes, the war is finally over."

EPILOGUE

NEW JERSEY

SEPTEMBER 1, 2009

UNITED STATES ARMY Chaplain Thaddeus Jones leaned back in the passenger seat and looked out the car window. The day was cool for early September, and as dusk deepened, lights started spilling out of neighborhood windows. Chaplain Jones had been in the army for twenty years and during that time he'd had his share of counseling irate married couples, had listened to the agonizing stories of young soldiers back from the battlefields and had consoled haunted, grizzled sergeants as they sat and wept in his study. However, in all of the years he had served, nothing bothered him as much as these visits, insofar as he was never the bearer of good news. He would, in fact, be coming to tell them their loved one would not be coming home. Insofar. He pondered the word and rolled it around on his tongue. What does it even mean, he wondered.

Lieutenant Eric DeFreeze, Branch Officer, turned into the driveway of the little Cape-style house in Atlantic Highlands and stopped; Chaplain Jones gave him a tired smile and opened the door. As they stepped from the brown government sedan they stopped, looked around, puzzled. The yard was overgrown, tomato plants withered at the side of the house. A lone bed sheet was flapping on a clothesline. Weeks' worth of newspapers cluttered the porch and the mailbox was filled with unopened mail and catalogs. They climbed the steps and Chaplain Jones noticed faded geraniums in copper pots, dry and dying. Except for one light in the kitchen, the house was dark. The door to the garage was closed tight, the overhead light dark. Chaplain Jones sighed with the burden of the news he brought and, smoothing his uniform, leaned over and pushed the doorbell. "I always hate this part of my responsibility," he said sadly. Inside the house, the bell rang and rang and rang.

At a window table in Adalet's Apron, Jena Rose took out her cell phone and called Rebecca Wade to let her know she was back from California.

And on the northern end of Sandy Hook, a sudden breeze sprung up with the setting sun. It swept across the empty seawall and picked up a paper cup, tumbling it down the bank and into the bay. It swept around Number 24 Officers' Row and shook the windows, banging a loose shutter and sending a dust devil spinning across the veranda. Inside the empty house a soft, blissful laugh broke the silence and then faded away.

AUTHOR'S NOTES

THIS IS A work of fiction based on an actual location but the characters and events are from my imagination. I have also taken a number of liberties with some of the descriptions of Fort Hancock, History House, Atlantic Highlands, the deployment of the New Jersey National Guard and Swansboro, North Carolina. For instance, in History House there is no office across from the kitchen, no blackboard with August 15 or any other dates and as Fort Hancock is part of the National Park Service, there would be no civilian guides. Additionally, History House is not haunted by a strange woman who walks the halls at night.